CHRISTMAS SECRETS

SECRETS OF THE HEART SERIES
BOOK 5

ELIZABETH ROSE

OLIVERHEBERBOOKS

Copyright © 2023 by Elizabeth Rose Krejcik

Published by Oliver-Heber Books

0 9 8 7 6 5 4 3 2 1

 Created with Vellum

CHAPTER ONE

"Percival, ye're never goin' to find a wife if ye dinna get out of this dark corner and go stand under the kissin' bough."

Percival Hamilton looked up from polishing his sword to see his sister-by-marriage Morag standing over him with her six-month-old baby daughter, Mazelina, latched to her hip. It was nearly Christmastide at Rothbury Castle, with the celebrations already starting even though Christmas was still three days away. The great hall was decorated with juniper boughs, holly, and those blasted conglomerations of mistletoe, grapevines, and a few things he couldn't decipher. The stupid things were hanging everywhere in the great hall. Morag called them kissing balls or boughs, or mayhap they were bogs. Percival wasn't really sure and neither did he care.

"I assure you, Morag, that I am not interested in finding a wife. However, when I am, I won't need your help." Mayhap he came across as sounding bitter, but Christmas wasn't his favorite time of year. Even after being released with the rest of his family from the dungeon of the evil Lord Whitmore, his nightmares of the past never seemed to end.

"Percival, ye havena even held Mazelina since she's been born. Here, take her." The pushy girl held out the child to him, but he held up his hands and shook his head. Why should he hold a child? He was a warrior and didn't walk around burping blasted babies. That was for women to do.

"Morag, if you need help with your daughter, I suggest you call for the nursemaid and not give her to me," snapped Percival.

She stiffened and pulled her baby back to her bosom as the child started to cry. "My nursemaid is with her family for Christmas. Besides, I don't need one."

"You are a lady. You are not supposed to be raising your own child."

"I like doing so. And Bedivere doesn't mind."

"It figures," he mumbled. "My brother wouldn't know anything about acting proper."

"Well neither do ye, or ye'd be callin' me Lady Morag instead of just Morag."

"You asked me to just call you Morag without your title, unless you've forgotten. But I assure you, it won't happen again, *Lady* Morag," he said to prove his point.

Looking down at his shiny sword, Percival saw his own reflection. His long blond hair was tied back, and he wore the clothes of a noble... but not of a knight. He also wore on his chest the crest of the Hamilton family, which was a sword wrapped in vines. His older brother, Bedivere, started wearing a different crest after marrying Morag. His family's crest had been replaced with a crown with three pieces from a chess game instead. A black bishop, knight, and rook were at the base of the crown, and in the center was a white king from the game. It was the crest created by Morag's father and uncles, who were the Legendary Bastards of the late King Edward III. King Richard, England's ruling sovereign, was Morag's half-cousin.

"Ye seem like ye're sulkin' or perhaps hidin' over here. I hope ye'll at least talk with my sister and cousins when they arrive."

"Lady Morag, I already know your sister Fia. I also know your cousins Willow and Maira. I really have nothing to say to them." The baby on Morag's hip fussed, and she jostled it up and down. "And once again, you are a lady, and shouldn't be carrying around a baby. Summon your nursemaid for that. Or at least call on my mother to help you."

"Nay," protested Morag in her normal stubborn manner. "Mazelina is my daughter, and I want to carry her as much as possible and spend time with her because she means the world to me."

"But that isn't the way of nobles," he reminded her once again.

"Bedivere and I want to have a bigger presence in our children's lives. We want to spend as much time as possible with any children we may have."

"And I would like to spend as much time possible away from babies, children, and celebrations having to do with Christmas." He glanced upward to the hanging ball-type object above Morag's head. "Especially those stupid kissing things." He stood up and used his sword to swipe above his head, severing the string holding the kissing bough above them, letting it fall to the ground.

Morag's eyes opened wide. "My sister and cousins helped

me to make those and hang them up for the Christmastide celebrations. How dare ye destroy it so carelessly!"

"It's naught but some branches and vines, so quit acting as if I've taken a life," said Percival, slipping his sword back into his sheath. "After all, I'm not Bedivere," he said under his breath, referring to the fact that his brother was once an assassin.

"Darling, there you are." Morag's husband, Bedivere, who was also Percival's brother, walked up and put his arm around Morag's shoulder. He looked down at the kissing bough at his feet. "I don't see a kissing bough above our heads, but I won't let that stop me."

Leaning over, he gave Morag a quick peck on the cheek. Then he stuck out his finger, letting the baby grip it. The little girl laughed.

"Mazelina, you are getting so strong," said Bedivere, making a face to pretend it hurt, managing to make the baby laugh even more. While Morag was half Scottish, Percival was an Englishman. Bedivere won a competition, therefore claiming the title of lord of Rothbury Castle, so this is where they now resided.

As far as Percival was concerned, his brother Bedivere had it all. Already a knight, and now a lord of one of the most prestigious castles in England, he also married a daughter of one of the Legendary Bastards of the Crown. He had started a family as well. Everything seemed to fall in his lap so easily lately. Percival wished that would happen to him.

"Brother, is this really acceptable behavior for a knight and lord of a castle?" Percival shook his head in disgust, nodding at Bedivere's actions.

Bedivere's gaze roamed over to Percival but he did

nothing to step away from Morag or the baby. "I don't remember asking your opinion on what I do. Neither do I think it is really any of your concern how I spend my time now that my life is mine again."

Percival knew exactly what he meant. "I suppose you think I should be bowing to you for saving our lives? Or mayhap you want me to pretend to be your squire like you did before."

Bedivere frowned. He took back his finger from the baby, kissing his daughter atop the head. Then he spoke to his wife. "Morag, why don't you take the baby to play with the other children. I'd like to speak to my brother alone."

"Of course," she said, first bending down and picking up the ruined kissing bough. "I'll have one of the servants fix this and hang it back up right away." She scowled at Percival and left the men.

As soon as she walked away, Bedivere stepped closer and spoke in hushed tones. "What the hell is the matter with you? And what has made you so grouchy? I've never seen you act like this. What is going on?"

"Me?" Percival blew a puff of air from his mouth and shook his head. "There is nothing wrong with me, Bedivere. After all, I'm not the one acting more like a wench than a man."

Bedivere's hand shot out to punch him, but Percival was quick and blocked the blow. He knew his brother well enough to be prepared for his reactions.

"Well, I see you learned something through all your training as a knight." Bedivere lowered his hand and let out a deep breath. "Why didn't you go through with being knighted? It is what Father would have wanted."

Just hearing his brother mention their father stirred the haunting memories in his head once again.

"Mayhap I don't want to be a knight, after all."

"What?" Bedivere's brows arched. "But it is what you've always wanted, Percival. You're so close to becoming one, and only need to go through with the knighting ceremony."

"Mayhap I'll be a mercenary instead."

"God's eyes! What are you saying?" This spurred Bedivere's anger.

"What's wrong with being a mercenary? I hear they make good money."

Bedivere narrowed his eyes. "It is nearly Christmas, Percival. I don't know what's got into you lately, but I want things to go smoothly at my castle during the holiday. I want everyone to be merry. I want men and women to sing and drink and even dance. I want the children to play and laugh. This is what Christmas is all about. Not brooding over something in the past. I don't want trouble. Do you understand? You need to smile and enjoy the upcoming holiday celebration. Get drunk. Bed a wench or mayhap two." He motioned with his hands as he spoke. "Stop being so serious and start living a little. Enjoy that you wake up in the morning and that you have a life to live."

"If I'm alive, why do I feel so dead inside?" asked Percival. "I swear, this is no different than being in Whitmore's dungeon."

"Don't say that! You know it's not true. Now, just relax, will you?"

"How can I relax when Morag is pestering me to find a wife, and you're forcing me to participate in events that mean nothing to me. The worst part is that I'm expected to kiss wenches under hanging balls!"

Bedivere chuckled. "Boughs. Kissing boughs is what they are called. And you need to take your ease, little brother. This is just what you need. I mean... how long has it been since you've even been with a woman?"

"That has nothing to do with it! I'm just... you just..." Percival shook his head and lowered his gaze to the floor, not finishing his sentence. "Forget it. You wouldn't understand."

"Go ahead. Please, speak freely. Let me try to understand you."

Percival's head snapped up and he spoke through gritted teeth. "Fine. I will speak freely. You disgust me, Bedivere. You've gotten so soft since you married Morag, that you will end up being the laughing stock of all England."

"What?" Bedivere frowned. "What does that mean?"

"God's eyes, Brother, our father was once a respected knight. At least you were respected too, even if it was as an assassin! People feared you. You were looked upon much differently then. Look at you now. Now you're kissing under hanging greenery and babbling senselessly to babies!"

This time, Percival grabbed Bedivere's wrist when the punch came close to his face. "See what I mean? I never could have warded off one of your punches before. No one could escape your skills of fighting or killing. You were one damned good assassin.

"Don't ever say that again! It is nothing I am proud of. Do you hear me?" Bedivere spoke through gritted teeth. "That is a part of my past that I don't ever want my children to hear about. It wasn't my choice, or did you forget?"

All of a sudden Percival felt shame overwhelm him. He

and his family had a horrible time after his father was convicted of plotting to kill the king, and hanged. Bedivere, on the other hand, was truly the one who saved them all from death. He was sure it couldn't have been easy to kill on command, especially when Bedivere didn't even know his targets until the last minute.

"You're right. I'm sorry, Bedivere." Percival pushed Bedivere's hand away. "If only Father were still alive, mayhap things would be different."

"He died at Christmastime. Is that what is bothering you?"

"I can't get the vision out of my head of seeing him swinging from that rope. And the mockery of Whitmore and his men was horrible. How demented of him to decorate the gallows with... with things like this." Percival raised his hands to include the festive decorations. "Christmastide isn't something I'll ever celebrate again. It only reminds me of death and suffering. That's all it'll ever be to me."

"Mayhap you should take a walk and clear your head," suggested Bedivere. "Don't let the demons of the past haunt you in such a way that it ends up ruling and ruining your life."

"I'll do better than that. I'm going hunting in the forest. I might be gone for a few days, or mayhap even until after Twelfth Night is over."

Bedivere cocked his head. "You can't run from yourself."

"I'm not."

"Aren't you? This has affected you so much that you are starting to resent my good fortune, and even turned down the opportunity to be knighted. For the life of me, I cannot figure out why you are acting this way."

"It doesn't matter. Nothing does. And my memories of the past cannot be erased by kissing wenches or getting soused."

"Nay. I don't suppose they can." Bedivere put a gentle hand on Percival's shoulder.

"How do you deal with your bad memories of the past?" asked Percival, not knowing how his brother could even sleep nights after having murdered nearly a dozen men.

"I make new memories to replace them," explained Bedivere. "That is, good Christmas memories to bring light to replace those dark times. Morag taught me how. That is what I do. I tell you, it really works." Bedivere looked over at Morag and the baby and flashed a quick smile when their eyes interlocked.

Percival groaned. "Mayhap I'll take you up on that idea of getting drunk after all." He snatched a bottle of wine from the tray of a passing server. "I'll stop in the kitchen and take some food along, too. I'm taking enough provisions to last me a week in case the hunt is not successful."

"Stop it," growled Bedivere, shaking his head. "Your home is here at the castle now. This is where you belong. Not living like a hermit in a cave somewhere."

"Don't you mean, *your* home?" Percival asked him.

"Rothbury Castle is home to my entire family now. All of us," he told him.

"Mayhap you're right. I need to create new memories like you've suggested. Goodbye, Brother." He headed for the kitchen.

"It's snowing out there. And the hunt is never successful this time of year and you know it." Bedivere hurried after him, talking as they walked. "You can't really mean to camp in the wilderness. You'll freeze to death."

"Well, at least it'll cool my heated temper as you suggested. Don't come looking for me, because I don't want to be found."

"At least take shelter somewhere."

Percival stopped in his tracks and looked back at his brother. "Shelter? Do you mean because we're so close to the Scottish border?"

"Well, it's not safe to be alone out in the woods and you know it. You're a target for any Scot wandering over the border looking for trouble."

"Don't worry about me. I know how to fight." He tapped the hilt of his sword at his side and started for the kitchen once again.

"Mother won't be happy when I tell her you won't be here with the rest of the family for Christmas. She'll also want me to go out and fetch you and bring you back home. And you know that is not what I want to be doing at Christmastime."

Percival stopped again, knowing this was true. And being the second eldest son, it was his responsibility as well to look after their mother and younger siblings. God's eyes, he didn't need this guilt laid on him right now. But he also couldn't stomach the idea that he might make his mother cry after all the hardships she'd been through.

"I don't want Mother to worry about me. Tell her I'll be staying in the cottage for a while and will be safe. I'll return soon." He spoke to Bedivere without turning to look at him.

"Cottage?" Bedivere stopped at his side. "Are you talking

about that run-down little hovel in the woods where Morag and the girls used to go to see that old woman?"

"Yes," answered Percival. "It is where they met with the old woman, Imanie. In that secret garden."

"Ah, you know about that then." Bedivere crossed his arms over his chest.

"Of course I do. Everyone does. They were members of a secret group of strong women started by the Queen, and even had little brooches they wore that looked like hearts. They were Followers of the Lonely Heart before they all married."

"Secret Heart," said Bedivere, cocking a half-smile. "But while you're there, you can start a new secret group called the Followers of Lonely Hearts since loneliness seems to be your problem lately." He chuckled at his jest.

"Not funny," said Percival, leaving his brother and heading off to the kitchen, feeling an emptiness in his heart that he couldn't explain. It was as if something was wrong and he didn't know how to fix it. Something was definitely missing in his life, but he wasn't sure what. But, hell, if Bedivere was right, saying Percival was lonely. He didn't know what he was talking about. Whatever it was making Percival feel so empty this time of year, it certainly had nothing at all to do with a lonely heart!

CHAPTER TWO

Holly Wakefielde slid off her horse and pushed open the old wooden gate to the secret garden. The snow fell faster now, and the flakes seemed even bigger. She felt relieved to have made it to her destination before the winter storm worsened. Or before they were caught.

It had been over five years now since she'd been here to the secret garden to visit her grandmother, Imanie. If she had been allowed to visit more often, she surely would have taken the opportunity to do so. Shame as well as excitement filled her being, wanting to see the old woman again after so long. Grandmother had never even met Holly's little brother, Noel. Nothing pleased Holly more than to think they'd be spending the Christmas holiday with the only family member they had left. This would be a special Christmas indeed. Noel was anxious to meet her, although he was still missing his mother. So was she.

"Grandmother, we're here! Grandmother, where are you?" Holly called out, her smile dying on her face when she eyed the snow-covered cottage and the frozen secret garden that surrounded it. The small wooden one-room home had a thatched roof and a small porch out front with three steps leading to the front door. It was surrounded by an enclosed garden with lots of trees and a wooden fence. Nestled away in the woods, not many people even knew this was here. Her grandmother even had a small barn off to the side with one stall for her horse. It was also where she'd kept all her tools to do her gardening.

While the place didn't look to be in really poor condition, something was different about it and definitely not right. She felt a loneliness in every bone in her body when this house and garden used to make her feel happy and so alive. Even though she couldn't understand it, she had the eerie feeling that this place was now uninhabited. Looking closer, she realized there was no smoke rising from a hearth inside the house. Also, the front steps were half-fallen down and the porch hadn't been swept at all and was filled with snow. Even the barn looked deserted with the door wide open and just darkness inside. She didn't see signs of life anywhere.

"I'm cold," complained her brother from atop the horse. Noel had just turned five years old yesterday. Holly would be more of a mother to him now than a sister, since the death of their mother two days ago. "I'm also hungry and I have to pee. Holly, I want Mother!"

"Oh, Noel, so do I, but you know she is gone from this earth now, and we are on our own." Holly walked back to the horse and reached up, helping her brother dismount, putting his feet on the ground. "As soon as we get inside, everything will be taken care of, I promise."

She held the hand of the little boy while she led the horse

over the frozen, desolate ground. Tall flowers were brown and wilted, falling over from being in the wind and snow. There were squares of earth with small fences around them that she remembered being used for vegetables and flowers of all kinds. Now, all they held were dead plants. Death was something she didn't want to feel right now.

The last time she and her mother were here, her mother had been pregnant with Noel. The secret garden, which was the home of her grandmother, had seemed like such a happy place then. Of course, it had been in the summer when everything was in full bloom. Beauty had flourished everywhere. Birds made their homes in the trees, and a trellis arched over an old wooden bench, filled with climbing, colorful roses. Holly remembered the bees and butterflies had flitted from flower to flower, and happily she had chased them through the mazes of magical-looking vegetation that her grandmother had so painstakingly tended to in order to make things perfect and special in this secret garden—this hidden place.

Leading the horse to the small barn, Holly entered to find it empty. There were no other animals anymore. At one time her grandmother had a horse and had even raised a few chickens, mainly for the eggs. She didn't understand why everything was so different. It all seemed so sad.

Her grandmother should be here. Things shouldn't seem so dreary. Even in the winter, Imanie had taken measures to keep up the grounds and decorate the cottage with juniper boughs and holly and trailing ivy wrapped around the railing on her porch. She even used to make fresh wreaths and hang them on her door.

Well, her horse wasn't here anymore. This wasn't a good sign at all. Where in the world could her grandmother be?

Holly was sure that her mother never would have sent her here if she thought Imanie had left. In all of her twenty-one years of life, Holly's happiest memories came from the few times she came here with her mother to visit her grandmother. It frightened her that she wasn't feeling that same happiness now. Now, she felt sad to be here and she didn't know why.

After stabling the horse, Holly led her brother up the broken, snow-covered stairs to the front door. Quickly knocking, she hurriedly put her hand back beneath her cloak for warmth. Even wearing traveling gloves, her fingers felt nearly frozen. Two days it had taken them to make the journey from Keswick in the storm when it should have taken no more than one. She hadn't even brought the wagon, not wanting to be slowed down or spotted by anyone. Sleeping on the ground last night in the woods had been colder and felt harder than even the thin straw pallets back at their hovel. She had lit a campfire to keep them warm, and thankfully it didn't give away their presence.

"Hello? Hello, is anyone home?" she called out, trying the door and finding it unlocked. She cautiously stepped inside the cottage, peering around the room, trying to get her eyes accustomed to the darkened area. Dust and mildew immediately assaulted her senses. As she entered farther into the room, her muscles clenched, already aching from the frigid air inside and the dampness of her surroundings. Something ran over her foot. She screamed and jumped, feeling her heart skipping against her ribs.

"Mousey," said the little boy happily, releasing her hand and chasing the rodent around the room trying to catch it and make it his pet. Noel loved all animals. Back home, while she and her mother had worked the land, Noel would occupy himself catching frogs at the creek, and chasing the birds. He even caught a baby rabbit one day, but Holly convinced him to put it back in the nest so its mother could raise it.

"Noel, stop running around," shouted Holly. "It's dark in here and hard to see. You're going to trip and fall." Thankfully, she spotted the hearth and knelt down to inspect it. There weren't a lot of logs, but still enough wood to start a small fire. Reaching into her bag, she retrieved her flint and knife, as well as some dried moss that she always carried with her to start a fire should she need it.

It took several tries, but she managed to light the hearth, the flames steadily growing higher to brighten the one-room cottage. Now, at least, there would be light enough for her to inspect the small home. Walking through the room, Holly removed her traveling gloves and ran her fingers over the dust covering the doors of the cupboard. She remembered how clean her grandmother Imanie had always kept this place. She used to tell Holly that no matter how small a home was, it didn't matter. It still deserved the proper attention, and to be clean and tidy. Never before now had Holly ever seen dust anywhere. Pulling open the cupboards one after another, she realized they were nearly empty. She did manage to find a few wooden cups and some bowls, but where was her grandmother's favorite ceramic platter, or the little covered box she used for special items, like putting her rings or pins inside? Holly used to feel like a princess when she peeked into the box and found jewelry that, to her, had looked like it belonged to a queen. Her grandmother used to tell her none of them really meant anything to her, except for the heart brooch she always wore that had been given to her by someone very special.

Inside a drawer, Holly discovered a handful of spoons and a large ladle. She even found a box of thread and needles that was once Imanie's sewing kit. These things all seemed to be abandoned. She could tell they hadn't been used in a long time.

Inspecting the place further, she realized there was no food at all to be found. Her stomach convulsed. They'd eaten most of what little they did have on the trip here. Had she known there'd be no grandmother or food when they arrived, she would have rationed the food a little more wisely. Now, with this winter storm, it wasn't even going to be plausible to think she could go out and hunt for a rabbit to fill their bellies. Dread washed through her, worrying for her little brother even more so than for herself.

Holly didn't see many of Imanie's personal belongings besides the sewing kit, a few aprons, and an old comb. No clothes, or books, or even her favorite wimple. Had her grandmother gone visiting for the holidays? Or perhaps moved? Nay, not likely. Imanie usually didn't like to go far. All her visitors, she'd told Holly, usually came to see her. Holly wasn't sure how that could be when this place was so hidden in the woods. Her grandmother was most mysterious at times. Now that Holly thought about it, so was her mother.

God's eyes, Holly hoped nothing had happened to her grandmother and that she wasn't gone for good. She was counting on the woman to take them in, now that they couldn't go back home and this would be their new home.

She glanced back over her shoulder to see her little brother pulling down his trews. "Wait! What are you doing?"

she shouted, thankfully spying a metal pan under the bed. She pulled it in place just in time for the boy to relieve himself into it.

"I'm hungry. And tired," said Noel with a yawn, wiping one sleepy eye with his fist. Holly pushed back a lock of his dark hair, so unlike her own bright blonde tresses.

Next, she helped him pull his trews back up and tie them in place. "I'll bring our things in, and give the horse some of the water and oats we brought with us. Then I'll find something for us to eat." She seriously wanted to cook the oats for themselves, but couldn't risk the horse dying on them or they'd really be in a bind. Picking up the bedpan to empty it outside, she headed for the door.

"Where is Grandmother?" asked Noel with another yawn. "You said she would make us fruit tarts."

Yes, Holly had promised her brother that, among many other things. But she was doing whatever it took, trying to get Noel to stop crying over the death of their mother. His crying would have only alerted the guards at Castle Kestwick. She hadn't even allowed herself to cry, because she knew she had to be strong now for her little brother. If they had been nobles, or even merchants, things would be so different right now. But they were only serfs. Having only a small portion of their own land, they had to work and farm the lord's land, giving him not only the crops they grew, but paying him taxes on top of that. Being a serf was a hard life. They were poor and lived in small hovels with dirt floors. Their homes were always cold, even with a fire burning. They had to get the lord of the castle's permission to marry, and were not allowed to leave without Lord Neville's approval as well. The evil lord very seldom gave that kind of permission, and when he did, it was only for a few days at a time. The last time they'd visited Imanie was only because Lord Neville's brother, Lord Henry, had convinced him to let them go. Lord Henry had been kind to her family in the past and her mother liked the man. This was probably the reason why his brother had sent him on long journeys overseas. Holly hadn't seen Lord Henry for quite a while now.

This time, in order to leave, she and her brother had to sneak out during the night. Thankfully, they hadn't been caught, or they'd have been punished severely. The last serf who was caught trying to escape was locked in the dungeon for a fortnight, then put in the pillory for a week while Lord Neville instructed everyone to throw rotten food at him. The poor serf almost froze to death since it had been winter. The man was warned that if he tried to escape again, next time he'd lose a finger or toe.

Nay, they weren't going back to Castle Keswick. Ever. Their mother was right in telling them to come here just before she died. Imanie was a strong and a good woman. She wasn't a serf, because the late Queen Philippa had taken a liking to her and brought her to the king's castle. If only she had brought the rest of her family along as well, things would be different and they'd have a better life.

Now, since escaping, what Holly and Noel had to do was to keep hidden for a year and a day. If they could stay out of sight and keep from being caught for that long, they would no longer be serfs, but be free. It seemed like such a long time. And now that they had no mother, no grandmother, and no food, it was going to seem much, much longer.

God's teeth, she prayed they hadn't been followed by any of Lord Neville's guards. Holly had left in such a rush in the middle of the night that she hadn't had time to take any of her belongings, let alone enough provisions for the two of them to survive. Then again, she had been counting on her grandmother giving them food and shelter. Obviously, that wasn't the case here anymore.

"I'm not sure where Grandmother is." Holly emptied the bed pan outside and came back to stoke the burning logs on the fire. "Until we get settled, why don't you lie down on the bed and take a little nap?" she told Noel. "You'll be much warmer under the covers."

"All right," said the little boy, still yawning as he pulled himself up onto the only bed and snuggled down under the covers.

Wrapping her cloak tighter around her and grabbing her gloves, Holly headed back out into the blowing snow. As soon as she'd descended the stairs, her attention was drawn to a knee-high piece of wood standing up under the trees off to the side of the cottage. Actually, there were two of them. Curiosity got the best of her. She trudged over, seeing the two planks clearly now. They were covered with snow, and backed up to a row of tall juniper bushes, but she was sure they were grave markers.

"Nay," she mumbled, part of her not wanting to look, but she had to know for sure. Bending over, she brushed off the snow on the first one. "Mazelina," she read aloud, recognizing the name of her mother's aunt. Holly had heard her mother talk about the woman but personally had never met her. Then, she brushed off the second plank, her action freezing when she saw her grandmother's name—Imanie—engraved upon it.

"Grandmother, nay!" she cried, falling to her knees in the

snow. "This can't be," she wailed, realizing that in her absence, she had lost two more family members. Finally, she released the tears she'd been holding back while trying to stay strong. Not only her mother, but now her grandmother too? This was the last of her family. Now, she and Noel were really on their own. This thought scared her more than anything in her life.

PERCIVAL STABLED HIS STEED, surprised to see another horse already within the stall. Then he looked out and saw smoke rising from Imanie's deserted cottage.

"What the hell," he grumbled, securing the horse and running his hand over her flanks. "I'll be right back, girl." Leaving his travel bag attached to the horse, he drew his sword and headed for the cottage. If someone was here, it was probably bandits or mayhap looters. No one else would be out here in this storm. Either way, they didn't belong here and he would see to it that they left, even if he had to fight them off or kill them. They didn't belong here. Besides, this was his dwelling from now through Twelfth Night. No one was going to take it from him. He'd see to that if it was the last thing he ever did.

Percival quietly let himself in, not wanting to alert the intruders. Then, with his back against the wall, he moved silently farther into the house with his sword in his hand. Sure enough, there was a fire on the hearth; however, he didn't see anyone present.

Curious, he scanned the rest of the one-room cottage, but all he found was a leather travel bag lying by the hearth. He was about to inspect it when he heard a small noise from the bed. Turning quickly, he noticed a mound of mussed covers with some furs thrown on top. He decided there might be a ruffian lying under all that bulk, in wait for him.

With one hand he ripped back the covers, pointing his sword right where he thought the intruder's throat would be. "Aha!" he shouted, then stopped and blinked when he realized a little boy was there sleeping. Slowly, the boy's eyes opened and then they became wide with fright.

"Nay! Holly!" he screamed, confusing Percival as to why he'd be calling out the name of one of Morag's silly holiday decorations instead of calling for help.

"Put down the sword or I'll run my blade right through you!" He heard a voice from behind him that sounded odd and too high. Then he felt the pinch of something at his back. He spun around, ready to break the intruder's neck. Reaching out, he brought the tip of his sword to the man's neck.

That is when he realized it wasn't a man at all. The intruder's hood fell back and he saw a short woman with a round face and red cheeks. Her long blonde hair was twisted into a braid that was flipped over one shoulder. Bright blue eyes stared up at him in alarm as he knocked the knife from her hand and it went sliding across the wooden floor.

"You're a girl," he said, still trying to comprehend this. Why the hell would a girl and a young boy be here in this weather?

"I am," she said. "And you've got a big sword pointed at my throat even though I am no longer armed." She glared at him, looking down the end of his blade.

"Oh. I'm sorry." He quickly lowered his sword, but to his

surprise she spun around and grabbed a chair and swung it at him next. He raised one arm to block the blow. The boy on the bed jumped onto his back, gripping Percival's hair in his fists and pulling hard.

"Leave us alone! If you try to hurt us, I swear I'll kill you," the woman threatened.

"I'll kill you, too!" cried the boy, now wrapping his arms around Percival's neck and squeezing hard while he kicked his stockinged feet against Percival's back.

"What the hell," Percival ground out, finding it hard to speak or even breathe in this position. The little whelp was digging his fingers in hard. He grabbed the chair and threw it across the room. Then he reached back and pulled the little boy off of his back, flinging him down on the bed.

That's when the woman rushed him, throwing herself at him, knocking him down on the bed next to the boy. Percival dropped his sword and twisted around to catch himself to keep from falling on and crushing the youngster. He ended up with the girl atop him now, her legs spread around him as she pounded her fists against his chest.

"Now, this is an interesting position to be in," he said with a chuckle, reaching out to grab her wrists in his hands to stop her. When the boy started to go for his hair again, he put both the girl's thin wrists into one of his hands and used his other hand to hold back the boy. "Who are you?" he asked the woman.

"Leave us alone," she cried, reaching out and biting his hand hard.

"Ow!" He pushed up on the bed, trapping the woman atop his lap, wrapping his other arm around the boy, putting the child in a headlock. Now, neither of his attackers could move.

"Please don't hurt us," begged the woman, squirming and finally going limp against him as she gave up the fight.

"Hurt you? Is that the way you see it?" he asked. "What I'm seeing here is the two of you trying to hurt *me*."

"Leave me and my sister alone or our grandmother is going to hurt you!" shouted the boy.

"Grandmother? Oh," he said, starting to understand. "Was Imanie your grandmother?"

"She still is. She's tough. That's what my sister said. Tell him, Holly. Tell him Grandmother won't let anyone hurt us." The boy wiggled and looked up from beneath Percival's arm.

When the woman remained silent, he slowly released her, but still kept the boy in a headlock.

"Yes, Imanie is... *was* our grandmother," said the blonde woman. "But I've just discovered her grave outside. Noel, I'm sorry, but Grandmother is dead."

CHAPTER THREE

"Please. Release my brother," Holly begged the man, taking the opportunity to get off his lap as soon as he slackened his hold.

"I'd be glad to, as long as the little whelp stops pulling my hair."

"Noel, leave the man alone," she scolded.

"And no more biting, either," added the man before Noel tried to bite him again.

"But he's trying to kill us," said Noel, squirming and looking up at Holly. He was so young but sometimes acted so brave that it made her smile inwardly. He was trying to protect her, and doing a good job at it too.

"I am not going to kill you or even hurt you." The man looked like a warrior and she wasn't sure she really believed this. Still, she and Noel were no match for an armed man.

"You claim you won't hurt us, but then why were you holding your sword to my brother when I walked in?" Holly boldly bent down and used both hands to pick up the man's blade at her feet. It was heavier than she thought it would be.

Although she wanted to point it at him in return, the tip fell and she found it hard to hold it outright at all.

"Give me that before you hurt someone." The man released Noel and jumped off the bed, yanking the sword away from her. She quickly moved away from him, her back now against the wall. "I told you, I'm not here to hurt anyone," he continued. He threw down his sword atop the table. "I thought you were thieves, that's all. I wasn't expecting to find anyone here, and you took me by surprise."

"Oh," Holly commented, swallowing the lump in her throat. Looking at his face this closely in the firelight, he no longer seemed so threatening, but almost kind. Actually, he was a very handsome man. He stood tall, his build medium, his blond hair hanging long and loose around his shoulders. It seemed as if it had been pulled back, but her brother probably yanked it loose in the fight. His eyes were a light green and almost seemed to glow in the firelight. Shadows fell over his sculptured face, making him look mysterious. She found herself curious and needed to know more about him. "So... who exactly are you?"

"Me?" His hand turned upward. "I'm Percival Hamilton. My brother is lord of Rothbury Castle. Who are you?"

"Percival Hamilton," she repeated, making her way slowly toward her brother. "I know for a fact that Lord Walter Beaufort is lord of Rothbury Castle. My grandmother told me so. He is quite old, and you are much too young to be his brother."

"Aye, you are right," Percival answered with a nod. "Lord Walter Beaufort was lord, but he died. My brother, Bedivere holds that title now."

She supposed this could be true, since she hadn't been

back to Rothbury in years now. "When did Imanie die?" she asked, her heart aching just to say the words aloud, admitting that her grandmother was really gone.

He seemed to think about it for a minute, scratching his head as he answered. "I'd have to say mayhap two or three years ago. I never knew her personally, but my sister-by-marriage did."

"Two or three years ago?" she mumbled. In deep thought, her fingers stroked the heart brooch that was clasped onto her cloak. Had things really changed that drastically over that short amount of time? Now she regretted not having had the chance to spend more time with Imanie.

She saw Percival's gaze go to her hand. "Ah, you're wearing one of those heart brooches like the girls wear. So you belong to the group as well," he surmised.

"Pardon me?"

His long finger pointed at the brooch holding closed her cloak.

"Lady Morag and her sister Fia, as well as their cousins, Maira and Willow, all have those. I hear Imanie had one too."

"Yes, the heart brooch," she said, looking down and rubbing her fingers over the pin once again. She remembered well that her grandmother used to wear one just like her mother. When she'd asked about them, she was told that when the time was right, they'd tell her more about them. It never made any sense to Holly. It seemed as if they had some kind of secret that they didn't want to share with her. She'd always loved the heart brooches, and asked for one as well. Her grandmother told her that those were given to them by the late Queen Philippa, but she wouldn't say any more. Now, the brooch was Holly's, and she cherished it even more than when she was young. This was the last remembrance she had of her mother.

"Ah, the brooch does change things," Percival observed. He also did something extremely odd and spoke from behind his hand. It was almost as if he were telling her some sort of secret.

"I'm sure I don't know what you mean."

"You don't need to keep it a secret from me. I know all about it."

"You do?" she asked, having no idea what he was talking about.

"You are part of that secret group of strong women. The one with those followers of the lonely hearts. I mean... secret hearts. Right?"

"I-I... if you say so." Her hand clutched the metal heart pin, as she now wondered exactly what her mother and grandmother had not told her. Secret group of strong women? This was the first time she'd ever heard something like this. The idea intrigued her.

When her mother gave the brooch to her on her deathbed, she also told Holly to take Noel and go live with their grandmother. She said the brooch would protect her as well and to never lose it or give it away. Holly dismissed the odd thing her mother said, thinking the poor woman was delirious with pain from the breathing illness that had come upon her and killed her so suddenly.

Thankfully, the rest of the serfs said they'd wait until morning to inform Lord Neville of her mother's death. They also promised to give her a Christian burial. What little money Holly had, she gave to her neighbors to pay the priest at the church to bury her mother. Her friends also said they would not tell Lord Neville that she and Noel ran away, but it wouldn't take long for him to notice they were missing. Holly prayed the rest of the serfs would not be punished for her leaving.

She followed her mother's dying wish and thankfully was able to find the cottage and the secret garden again after all this time.

Lord Percival continued. "I suppose you'll be disappointed to know that the secret group dissolved after the death of the old woman and when the rest of the followers either got killed off or married."

"Killed off?" she asked, not liking the sound of this.

"Or, at least that is what I've heard." He chuckled. "After all, it was a group of women, so I guess you never know for sure what really happened. They were said to have been chosen for the group because they were strong." He perused her up and down, making her feel a little uncomfortable. "You seem like a strong woman, so I understand now why you tried to attack me."

"I wasn't attacking you, I was defending my brother," she corrected him. Holly was tiny and far from strong. Therefore, he must mean strong in other ways besides being physical. She wanted to know more about this secret group of strong women he spoke of, but decided now wouldn't be a good time to ask. He almost seemed to respect her now because he thought she was someone who she obviously wasn't. Therefore, she'd let him think what he wanted, and hopefully it would keep her and her brother safe after all.

"What are you doing here, Sir Percival?" she asked him. "This is not a close walk from the castle, and we are in the midst of a blizzard."

"Oh, no need to call me Sir," he told her. "I am... I am not a knight."

"You're not?" Her eyes went back to his sword. "Then are you perhaps a castle guard?"

"Nay. Nay, I'm not."

"Please, don't tell me you're a mercenary?" She made it over to her little brother, pulling him to her in a protective hug as he stood next to her atop the bed.

WHEN PERCIVAL SAW the look of disgust and horror on the girl's face when she asked if he was a mercenary, he found himself tongue-tied and unable to speak. When he told Bedivere earlier he was going off to be a mercenary, the idea hadn't seemed so bad. As a matter of fact, it had felt freeing and adventurous, not to mention it wasn't bad pay. But now, after seeing Holly's expression, he felt horrible. The girl seemed to fear him. He'd thought to be feared was a good thing. If so, why didn't this feel good at all? He would never tell her that it was exactly what he'd planned to do. Percival's stomach twisted into a knot. Was this how Bedivere felt when Percival had called him an assassin? But that was different, he reminded himself. His brother really had been an assassin. Percival had only flirted with the idea of becoming a mercenary.

"I'm a... a noble," he told her, choosing his words carefully. After all, it would do no good to scare a woman and child. He wanted them to feel comfortable around him, not frightened. Yes, he decided he would do whatever it took to make them relax. "I've completed my training to become a knight, but just haven't been knighted yet and taken my vows."

"I see." The girl blinked her long lashes, staring at him, making him feel like some kind of liar.

But it wasn't a lie. It was exactly what really happened. Of course, he didn't offer the information that he'd turned down the chance to be knighted for reasons that she'd never understand.

"Please, don't make us leave here," begged the girl.

"You want to stay? Here in this broken-down cottage, away from everyone?" He splayed out his arms to include the surroundings.

"The truth is, we have nowhere else to go."

"Why not? Where are you from? Are you a titled lady perhaps, traveling in disguise for some reason?" He found himself curious about the girl, wanting to know more.

"Nay. I am not a noble, my lord," she said, using his title, even if she didn't realize it was only a courtesy title, and he held no lands.

"The daughter of a merchant, perhaps?"

"Nay. I... our mother just died. My brother and I were coming to stay with my grandmother—the only relative we had left. Well, besides my aunt, but I saw her gravestone out in the garden as well."

"I'm sorry," said Percival, really meaning it. "So, you lived in a town then? Won't the lord of the castle who rules over the town take care of you now?"

Her eyes darted over to her brother and she pulled him closer, running a hand over his hair. "My brother is tired and hungry. It is getting dark and I need to unpack our things and tend to the horse yet."

"Of course. I understand," said Percival.

"If you'd be kind enough to leave now, I have a lot to do."

His head jerked upward. "Leave?" She was dismissing him, a noble, when she was naught but a commoner? He didn't like that in the least. Instead of going out the door, he picked up the chair she'd thrown at him and sat down on it, propping his feet up on the table next to his sword. "I'm not going anywhere," he told her. "Indeed, I'll be staying here at the cottage until after Twelfth Night."

"Twelfth Night? That long?" Her eyes opened wide. "Nay. Nay, that isn't possible." She took her brother by the hand and hurried over to stoke the dying fire. "We will be living here now, so you'll just have to go back to the castle or find somewhere else to stay."

The flames had eagerly eaten up what little wood was on the hearth. She kneeled down, blowing on the dying embers trying to bring it back to life.

"I'm really cold, Holly," said the boy, wrapping his arms around himself. His teeth chattered.

"Do you have food?" asked Percival, watching her try to fan the fire, but to no avail.

"I have a loaf of bread and some cider in my travel bag."

"And how long do you think that will last?"

"I-I don't know," she said, looking flustered as smoke started to fill the room.

"Allow me," he said, walking over and hunkering down, rearranging the burnt logs that were left, and easily bringing the fire back to life."

"That's warmer already," said Noel, getting closer to the flame and holding out his hands.

"Thank you, Lord Percival." When she looked back at

him over her shoulder, her bright blue eyes held such a sadness, yet at the same time gratitude. She seemed guarded, and as if she were holding back when she wanted to cry out. This girl was mysterious and he didn't understand her.

"You can't stay here alone with the boy." He stood up and walked back to the table and picked up his sword. "It's not safe. We're close to the Scottish border. Highlanders have showed up here before."

"They have?" She stood up so fast that she knocked into her brother and had to grab him so he wouldn't fall.

"Holly, I'm hungry. When are we going to eat?" whined Noel.

"Stay by the fire," she told her brother, getting a blanket off the bed and wrapping it around him. "I'll go out to the barn and collect our things and bring back our food. Then I'll go search for more wood for the fire."

"And who will be here to protect the boy while you're out looking for dry wood in a snowstorm?" asked Percival, sheathing his sword.

"I-I don't know. I guess I hadn't thought about that." Her eyes flashed back up to him. "Could you stay here with Noel until I return?"

"Me?" He released a puff of air from his mouth. "You just met me. Moments ago you thought I was going to hurt you, and now you want me to stay with the boy?"

"You said you wouldn't hurt us." She looked at him suspiciously. "That wasn't a lie, was it?"

"Nay, it's the truth. However, I'm sorry, I won't stay here playing nursemaid to a child. It's beneath me."

"Then I'll take him with me." Her defiant chin lifted into

the air. She looked so determined to actually do this that it almost made him laugh aloud.

"Holly—that's your name, isn't it?"

"It is. Holly Wakefielde."

"And I'm Noel Wakefielde," said the little boy, sounding like he wanted to be included. Holly oddly looked the other way when her brother said it.

"You stay here and I'll fetch your things and take care of the horses as well," offered Percival. "I know where the old lady stored a lot of extra dry wood for the winter, and I believe there is some left. I'll bring it back with me when I return."

"Y-you will?" she asked. "You'd do us this favor? But you don't even know us."

"Oh, it's not a favor," he made sure to tell her. "I'll require something in return."

He watched her grip the neck of her cloak so tight that her fingers turned white.

"I am not willing to agree to that kind of favor, my lord." The look of disgust was back on her face again.

"What kind?" he challenged her, watching her squirm, knowing exactly what she thought he meant and not correcting her.

"I am not that kind of girl!" She couldn't even look at him now.

"You really don't know how to cook?" he asked, watching her surprised expression as her gaze shot back to him.

"Pardon me, my lord?"

"Cook. Can you cook?" he asked.

"Why, yes I can."

"Good. That's all I require in return. A hot meal. I've

brought provisions. I have enough to feed myself for a few days. I'd be willing to share it with you and the boy. I just want you to warm up some food while I tend to the other chores, because I'll be damned cold by the time I return."

"Of course," she said, ever so softly. He swore he saw a stain of blush rise to her cheeks.

"My sister is a good cook!" said Noel with a smile. Then his smile slowly faded. "But she doesn't know how to make fruit tarts like Mother used to make. She promised that Grandmother would make them for me, but now Grandmother is dead too." He sniffled and wiped a tear from his eye. "I want Mother."

"Noel, we'll talk about all this later," said Holly, removing her cloak and hanging it on a hook on the wall. She looked back at Percival. "I'll cook for you, Lord Percival. And you can stay here until the storm lets up. However, you must promise to leave as soon as the weather clears. You must also promise never to lay a hand on me or my brother."

He chuckled inwardly, thinking how silly this girl was, trying to make deals like this when she was powerless to do anything to stop him from doing whatever the hell he pleased.

"Your grandmother might have lived here at one time, Holly Wakefielde, but remember, this cottage is on land that belongs to my brother. He knows that I will be staying here during Christmastide, so I'm not leaving. Therefore, my dear, you will do as I say, or you and your brother will be out in the snow looking for a place to live."

With that, he turned and left the room, hearing no argument at all from behind him.

CHAPTER FOUR

Percival returned to the cottage after unpacking Holly's belongings, bringing in his own things, and tending to the horses. He also gathered more dry wood that he found stacked in a corner in the barn.

"Mmmm, something smells good," he remarked, entering the cottage with his arms loaded down with the logs. He held so many that he could barely see over the top of the stack. After using his foot to close the door, he headed over to the hearth, stacking the logs by the fire. "This should be enough to hold us for a while. Plus, there is still more dry wood in the barn to last another day or two. As soon as the storm lets up, I'll search the woods for more."

Brushing off his hands, he stood and turned around to get his first look at the table. "What's this?" he asked, seeing a red piece of cloth covering the old wooden table. There were wooden dishes for the three of them set, filled with food. In the center of the table was a green lit taper candle stuck into the neck of an old dusty bottle. And around the centerpiece were fresh cut juniper boughs and even a few sprigs of holly. The scent of the greens mixed with food filled the air.

"The meal is ready. Sit down and eat." Holly nodded at the table. "Noel, come join us for some food, please." She used the iron poker to lift a pot with a wire handle off the fire. She placed it atop a flat stone on the table and used a ladle to scoop out the liquid and place it into the three wooden cups.

Percival removed his cloak and hung it on a hook, hesitant to sit at the table.

"What is that?" he asked, still standing there dumfounded. This table looked much too festive for him. And it only reminded him of his dreaded Christmas memories that he'd been trying so hard to avoid.

"I know what it is!" exclaimed Noel, crawling atop a chair. "Holly made my favorite drink. It's hot apple cider with cinnamon."

"She did?" He didn't quite know what to say.

"It's just cider warmed up over the fire." She placed down a cup in front of Noel, and when he got to his knees on the chair eagerly grabbing for it, she stopped him. "Careful, it's hot," she told the little boy. "Remember to blow on it first."

"I will," said Noel, sliding the cup closer, blowing before it even got near.

"Did he say cinnamon? I don't remember bringing any spices from the castle," said Percival, purposely not taking anything with him that would remind him of the holiday.

"Oh, I brought that with me, as well as this red square of cloth that my mother used to cover the table at Christmas. It doubles as a blanket at other times of the year," Holly told him, placing one cup at his place setting and the other in front of hers. "Cinnamon sticks are something we always have back home, even when it isn't a holiday."

"Really," he said, confused, wondering how a mere commoner would have enjoyed something usually used only by the nobles. "I thought you said you weren't noble."

"I'm not."

"Then how did you get a hold of such an exotic spice?"

"My mother was sometimes paid in food instead of coin for her services."

"Services?" He started wondering exactly what those services were.

"I'm speaking of her skill. She helped with birthing babies and assisted in healing the ill. She had a real talent with it and was called upon by many for her services. Even the nobles wanted her, once they heard what she could do."

"Oh, your mother was a midwife," he said, but she changed the conversation.

Holly sat down, looked at the candle, and smiled. "This candle came from a noble as payment as well. Lord Henry gave it to her when his wife died about six or seven years ago. For some reason, she never burned it."

"What? Your mother was rewarded at the death of a noblewoman?"

"Oh, nay! Lord Henry had caught the illness from his wife, and my mother was able to heal him. If he had called upon her sooner, she may have been able to save his wife as well, but he waited too long."

"I see. I figured it was from a noble," he said, since wax candles were something that only the clergy or nobles would have.

"This table isn't much, but I intend on making things

even more festive around here in the next few days. I want it to feel like a special Christmas." She looked over at her brother and smiled at him.

"Nay!" grunted Percival.

Her brows dipped. "Nay, what?"

"No more festive anything. I don't like festivals and I hate holidays and decorations. There's no need for that kind of nonsense."

"Not all of us think it's nonsense. How can you even say that?" she asked. "This is a spirit that accompanies Christmas that warms the hearts of men and lightens everyone's burdens."

"Mmph," he muttered. "Some burdens can never be lightened."

"What do you mean? Is something troubling you, my lord?"

"That's my business." He felt ready to explode. What was happening here?

"Lord Percival, please sit down," she said with a wave of her hand. "The food is getting cold. I warmed up the pork I found in your travel bag and made a sauce out of the dried currants and some ale and honey. I think it'll compliment the carrots and parsnips I found in your things as well."

"We brought the bread," said little Noel, pushing the hard loaf of brown bread over to him. "We're sharing. Don't you want any of our food?"

Percival slowly took a seat at the table. The last thing he wanted was any hard, brown bread. Being a noble, he was used to white bread at the table. But a part of him didn't want to disappoint the little boy. Slowly, he reached out, tearing off a piece of bread and handing it to Noel.

"Nay. I want you to have mine," said the child, for some reason almost melting Percival's heart with the child's innocent generosity, wanting to share what little he had.

"We will all share." Percival pulled off another piece for Holly and saved the smallest for himself. It was chewy, but he didn't complain. He also loved the flavors that Holly cooked up, having planned on just eating his food cold, actually.

"My lord, is it to your liking?" she asked.

"Yes. Very tasty." His eyes fastened to the flame on the taper as he ate. Then his gaze traveled down to the green branches and sprigs of holly on the table. His chewing stopped. All he could see in his mind was his father being led to the gallows. Everyone laughed and mocked him, having decorated the gallows with these exact things. They even had Christmas tapers burning on the platform, mocking his father, telling him to enjoy his Christmas.

This was more than he could handle. The scent of juniper was strong and he felt as if he were standing at the foot of the platform watching his father hang all over again.

He pushed up from the table so fast, he almost knocked it over.

HOLLY GRABBED for the candle as the bottle started to roll. All their dishes were spewed about as Percival shot out of his chair as if he'd been burned.

"I said no decorations!" he shouted, scooping up the boughs and holly sprigs, storming over to the door and throwing them outside.

Noel started to cry.

"Everything's all right, Noel." Holly quickly blew out the candle and hurried over to her brother. "It's been a long day. You get to sleep and I'll join you shortly."

After tucking the little boy in, she pulled a curtain across that was fastened to the ceiling. This gave the person in the bed a little privacy.

A cold breeze blew into the cottage along with snow. When she went to close the door, she noticed Percival standing on the porch without his cloak. He had his face buried in his hands.

"Is something the matter?" she asked softly.

"Leave me alone," came his gruff reply.

"Why don't you come back into the cottage where it's warm."

His hands came away from his face. "I said, leave me alone, dammit." He stormed off for the stable.

Holly watched him go. She was tempted to follow, but didn't want to upset him more than he already was. She wasn't sure if she did something wrong. She didn't think so. Still, the man's demeanor changed so quickly that she was starting to wonder again if it was safe to stay in the cottage with him.

She finished cleaning up the dishes and put more logs on the fire. Still, Percival hadn't come back into the house. All she wanted to do was to climb in bed next to Noel and sleep. But she couldn't. Not when she knew Percival was out there in the cold.

Donning her cloak, she grabbed his cloak from the hook on the wall. It was a warm cloak made of wool and lined with ermine. Still, she took one of the extra blankets off the bed and headed for the stable.

The wind whipped around her and the snow continued to fall. She felt frozen by the time she got to the stable. She was afraid she'd find him lying dead and frozen on the ground. But when she walked into the barn, she saw a light flickering from the other end.

"Percival?" she called out, but he didn't answer. She entered the stable and closed the door behind her, heading over to investigate the light. To her surprise, there was a small fire burning, enclosed in an iron pot. The smoke went up and out a small hole in the roof.

She smiled to herself. This man was handy. The area was warm and the horses neighed happily, munching on some old hay making her wonder where he'd found it.

Then she saw Percival. He was hunkered down in a stall with his arms crossed over his chest and a half-empty bottle of wine in his hand. His head was back against the wall. It looked as if he were trying to keep warm. And he was sleeping.

She wanted to wake him and tell him to come inside. Then again, she didn't want him to get grouchy again, especially since it looked as if he'd been drinking. Whatever it was that was bothering him, mayhap sleeping it off was the best answer.

She gently removed the bottle from his hand and he stirred but did not open his eyes. Then, she put it down and covered him with both his cloak and the blanket.

"Sweet dreams, my lord," she whispered, leaving him to his slumber, heading back into the house. Mayhap tomorrow she could persuade him to tell her what she did to make him so angry.

CHAPTER FIVE

P ercival awoke the next morning to the sound of pounding, not able to determine what he was listening to. He also couldn't figure out why he was so warm when he knew the fire had gone out hours ago.

He opened his eyes to find a blanket covering him. When he removed it, his cloak was over him too.

"Holly," he said with a grin. She must have come looking for him last night and covered him up. That touched his heart. No one had cared about him like this before. Holly was a stranger to him, yet her kindness went far beyond what was expected from just a peasant.

He stood up and stretched, still hearing the pounding in the distance. When he took a step he almost kicked over the half-empty bottle of wine. Holly. Again. She didn't have to leave it there with him, but she had.

He donned his cloak, folded up the blanket, and carried it with the bottle of wine out of the stable. That's when he saw Holly banging on the front porch stairs. There was a broom at her side. Little Noel stood next to her, watching what she was doing.

"Good morning," he said, startling her as he walked up behind them.

"Oh!" She spun around and dropped the iron poker from the fire. "You scared me."

"It looks like the storm broke," he said, glancing up at the sky. The winds had died down and it was no longer snowing. A murky tint of gray colored the sky, but he swore he saw a small patch of blue peeking through the clouds. "What are you doing?"

"I tripped on the broken step so Holly and I are fixing it." Noel held up the metal soup ladle.

"With that?" Percival shook his head and chuckled.

"I couldn't find a hammer, so I'm using the end of the poker to try to pry up the wood from the stair."

"Is that what all the noise is about?"

Holly stood up and wiped the back of her hand over her brow. "How did you sleep?" she asked.

"Thanks to a little fairy bringing blankets and cloaks, I'd have to say pretty good."

"That was my sister, not a fairy," said Noel, looking at Percival as if he thought he was stupid.

"I didn't want to disturb you, so I left the blanket and didn't wake you," explained Holly. In the morning light, Percival looked downright sexy. He had been clean-shaven yesterday with a smooth jaw. Today, he had stubble on his chin and cheeks, making him look rugged. She liked it. "I'm surprised you didn't sleep even later." Her eyes fastened to the bottle in his hand, subtly letting him know what she meant.

"Well, the pounding in my head woke me."

"Really?" She wiped her hand across her nose and stood up straighter. "That's only wine. I'd hate to think how much pounding there would have been in your head if you'd had whisky."

"I meant your pounding. On the stairs," he said raising his brows.

"Oh, that. Sorry." She smiled, now wanting to tell him she purposely pounded, wanting him to get up.

"I think I almost have the top of this step loose." With her hands on her hips, she looked at the stairs. When she turned back, he was standing very close to her. Her eyes interlocked with his. Oh, why did he look so handsome? She didn't want to like him. Not really. But if not, why was her focus on his mouth right now and why was she hoping for a kiss?

He reached out and lifted her chin with two fingers. Her eyes flashed upward. Immediately, she found herself drowning within the complicated depths of his clear orbs. He moved closer. She didn't budge. And just when she was sure he would kiss her, Noel said something and ruined the moment.

"I want to try now, Holly." The boy grabbed the poker from her hand, making Holly feel quite awkward. Would she really have kissed this man—this virtual stranger—with her little brother watching? And would he really try to make a move on her with a child present?

"You have dirt on your nose." He brushed it away with his thumb, cleared his throat and took a step backward. "Noel, let me help you with that."

Just using his hands for leverage, along with his legs, Percival was able to rip the top board off of the stair.

"Wow, you're strong!" said Noel with wide eyes. "I bet you could even pick up a horse."

"Well, I don't know about that, but I'll bet I could pick up a little boy." He threw down the board and scooped up Noel, holding him high over his head. Noel dropped the poker, nearly hitting Percival on the foot.

"This is fun! Look, Holly, I'm flying." Noel put out his arms to the sides, pretending he was a bird, flapping wildly, almost hitting Percival in the face.

Holly's heart soared. It was so good to see her brother laughing and smiling. Especially since they'd just lost their mother. Noel didn't have a father in his life. It did the boy good to have a man to mentor him. Or at least play with him in this manner and make him smile.

"That's enough, Noe," said Percival, putting the boy down.

"My name is Noel, not No," he complained.

"No, it's Noe," said Percival.

"No, it's not."

"Oh, it's Not? I thought it was Noe since there is No L in your name." Percival reached out and ruffled the boy's hair.

"That's funny," said Noel, sniffling and wiping his nose with the back of his hand. "Let's play another game."

"Mayhap later. Right now, I have a stair to fix." Percival picked up the board and inspected it, taking it with him as he headed for the barn.

"Noel, go inside. It's cold out and you're already sniffling. I'll be there soon," Holly told him. "I'm going to help Percival fix the stair."

"Huh?" Percival stopped and turned to look at her.

"I mean, Lord Percival," she corrected herself, not wanting to make him upset again.

"I'll start getting some ivy and juniper boughs together to make a wreath for the door." Noel jumped over the broken step and ran into the house.

"You do that," she mumbled, hurrying after Percival who had somehow already made it to the barn. God's eyes, he had long legs and an even longer stride!

She followed him inside, stopping next to him. He was on his knees digging through an old trunk.

"What are you doing?"

"I thought there were some gardening tools in here some-where." He rummaged through some things in the trunk.

"You're going to garden? In the snow?"

"Nay. My family has a nun and a girl named Hazel who keep up the grounds here since Imanie died. However, I don't think they come in the winter. Oh, here we are."

He stood up with a pair of shears in one hand, a hammer in the other.

"Garden shears? For what?" she asked with a giggle.

"For taking the nails out of the board. Which is your job, by the way." He handed her the shears.

"All right," she said, looking oddly at the shears, wondering just what he wanted her to do with them.

"Let me show you." He put the board on a bench, using his foot to keep it still. The nails stuck up in the air. "These nails are no good. They're bent. So, use the shears to snip them off flush to the board."

"I've never done this before."

"Like this." He pulled her over to him, tucking her in up against his chest to get his arm around her. He placed his hand over hers to demonstrate. The feel of his hot skin touching hers sent a delightful shiver up her spine. "Grab, twist, and pull. It pops right off. See?"

She would have seen if she had been watching. Instead she was looking up at him, and once again their faces were very close.

"I see." Her eyes drank him in, her gaze stopping at his mouth again as she looked at him over her shoulder.

"Do you," he said. "Then you'll see this as well."

Before she could ask what he meant, he leaned over and kissed her right on the mouth. It surprised her, as well as the fact that he let the kiss linger.

"I'm sorry," he whispered. "You wanted me to promise not to touch you," he said in a deep, sexy voice. She turned to face him and he cradled her chin with his large hand.

"You don't need to keep that promise." She raised her chin slightly, inviting another kiss.

"I don't believe I ever made the promise in the first place." His eyes were on her lips now.

"Nay," she answered in a breathy tone. "I guess you didn't."

You are a very beautiful woman, Holly." He ran a hand over her braid that was tossed over one shoulder, trailing down the front of her. She swore she felt a tingle of excitement wash through her when the tips of his fingers gently grazed one breast. Then he kissed her again, and she let him. Her hands raised up and rested on his sturdy chest. His lips felt surprisingly soft, and warm. And then to her astonishment, the kiss deepened and she felt his tongue slip in between her lips.

"Oh!" She broke the kiss, holding a hand over her mouth, quickly stepping away.

"What's the matter?" he asked. "Didn't you like that?"

"I did," she admitted. "But it surprised me."

"Oh, you haven't been kissed by a man before, I understand."

"Not in that manner." It was the truth. Her experience with men ended with a few kisses from one of the peasant boys where she lived when he decided to try to put his hand down her bodice. Her little brother had been watching, so she slapped the boy and he never tried anything with her again. Even so, those kisses were hard and cold and fast. They were nothing at all like what she'd just experienced with Lord Percival. His kisses made her feel special. His words made her feel pretty.

"Well, that's that," he said, quickly removing the rest of the nails and looking around. "I don't have the supplies I need to fix this. The horse needs to run, so I'll take a ride back to the castle to get what I need."

"You're leaving?" she asked, feeling her heart speeding up. She didn't want him to go. Not now. Not when he'd just kissed her. He couldn't leave now!

"You and the boy can join me. Go get him, but hurry. I want to get back before it starts snowing again."

"Go with you? To the castle?" Sudden fear overtook her. What if Lord Neville showed up asking questions and looking for her and Noel? As much as she'd love to spend Christmastide at the castle, she couldn't. It was much too risky. She needed to keep Noel safe. It was crucial they remain hidden.

"Sure. I will introduce you to my family," he offered, his invitation sounding so nice that she wished she could oblige.

"Oh, so you have a big family then?" she asked, stalling for time. She wasn't sure how to say no without telling him her reasoning. "Do you have more brothers besides Bedivere?"

"Bedivere is the eldest, and our twin brothers, Luther and Avery, are the youngest. They are a few years older than Noel."

"Oh, twins. That's nice. Four boys."

"And five girls," he added, preparing his horse to go.

"Five... more? Really?"

"Yes. Elizabeth, Avalina, Sarah, Claire, and Rhoslyn."

"That's a big family!"

"And there's my mother Ada, of course." He looked up in the air in thought. "As well as Aunt Joan and Uncle Theobald, who is half blind and some say crazy." He chuckled and pulled the straps tighter that secured the saddle.

"Is that all?" she asked in a jesting manner.

"Well, there is my sister-by-marriage, her baby, and her sister and cousins and their husbands and families, but I won't bore you with that."

"You mentioned everyone but your father it seems. What about him?"

Suddenly, his smile faded and he didn't look happy anymore. He fussed with the saddle, not looking at her when he spoke.

"My father is dead. He died on Christmas."

"Oh, nay. I'm so sorry," she told him, walking over and resting her hand on his arm. "How did he die?"

Dead silence. This was no doubt a sore spot, so she decided not to push him. "My mother just died too. From a breathing ailment."

"I'm sorry." He finally looked up. "What about your father?"

"He died in an accident plowing a field when I was only five."

"Plowing?"

"Helping a friend," she said, not wanting him to ask more about what they did. "He was kicked by a horse. Actually, this horse, right here." She pointed to her horse and he grimaced.

"And yet you didn't shoot the damned thing?"

"Why should we?" she asked. "It was an accident. The horse didn't mean to kick him. The mare's leg got caught in a rope and it spooked her."

"If I were you, the first thing I'd do is kill the damned animal that took my father's life." His entire face changed and he seemed so vengeful all of a sudden.

"I never even got the chance to know my father. My mother never remarried, so it was just the two of us for a long time until Noel came along."

"What?" He squinted and made a face. "So who is Noel's father?" he asked, making Holly want to bite her tongue. She didn't mean to tell him all that information. And she hoped that Noel would never know. And as far as Noel knew, her father was his, and that's the way her mother wanted it.

"Noel is... he's a bastard. But I don't want to tell him until he is older."

"Why didn't the damned man who planted his seed in your mother marry her, as is proper?"

These were too many questions. Questions she didn't want to answer. She didn't mean to say anything else, but just blurted it out before she could hold her tongue.

"My mother was taken against her will."

His head jerked upward. "By a bandit?"

"Nay. But he was a married man, so he couldn't marry her. Don't you understand?"

"Nay, not really. "You should have gone to the lord of the castle and relayed the story and he would have flogged the man or killed him. I know that is what my brother would do in a case like that. He is the deciding factor whenever there is trouble in town or on his demesne."

"I better go check on Noel." She turned to leave, but he grabbed her hand and spun her around.

"What's the matter, Holly?"

"Nothing. Why?" She tried her best to fake a small smile.

"You seem very upset about something."

"So did you last night when you almost knocked over the table in such a hurry to throw out my festive decorations."

"I told you, I don't like them and don't want them around me." He mounted his horse. "Now, are you coming to the castle or not? Your horse needs to run. I figure we'll feed and water them at the castle stable while we're there."

"Nay. I'm going to stay here with Noel."

"You cannot just let the horse stand and not feed it."

"Please, take my horse with you."

"But that will leave you with no form of transportation should you need to leave."

"I told you, I'm not going anywhere. My grandmother's cottage in her secret garden is my new home now."

"I wouldn't count on that," he muttered, reaching over

and untying the reins of her horse. "Well, stay inside until I return and lock the door. Don't open it for anyone."

"I'll be fine. We'll be fine," she told him, wrapping her arms around herself, almost feeling panicked that he was about to leave and taking her horse with him. If guards from Castle Keswick showed up searching for her and Noel, there would be no way she'd be able to escape them now.

"Hurry back," she called out as he left with the horses, already missing Lord Percival as soon as he rode out the gate of Imanie's secret garden.

CHAPTER SIX

"So, Brother, you've returned. I knew you would."

Percival groaned when he heard his brother's voice. Bedivere happened to be in the stables when Percival arrived at Rothbury Castle. Not at all what he'd been hoping for. Percival wanted to feed and water the horses, then collect some food from the kitchen and be on his way before anyone saw him. It was still early and he hoped not to see any nobles, at least. Now, he'd have to answer his brother's questions when that was the last thing he wanted to do.

"I'm surprised you're already up for the day, Bedivere." Percival dismounted. "After all, I know how you like to sleep late. Or should I say stay in bed with Morag?"

"Actually, I do. However, I was on my way to find you and bring you back for before Christmastide tomorrow. It was Mother's request."

"Of course." Percival handed over the horses to the stable boy, giving him instructions to feed and brush them. "Do it quickly," he said. "I'll be leaving again very soon."

"Where did you get a second horse?" Bedivere walked over to inspect it.

"It's not mine. I'm just tending to it for... a friend."

"A friend," repeated Bedivere, petting the horse on the nose and turning back to Percival. "Which friend? Who?"

"Never mind. It's not important."

"It seems important enough to bring the horse along with you, which tells me wherever you're staying, there are no provisions and you need to feed the horses."

"Don't even tell Mother I was here. I'm leaving again as soon as I replenish my food supply and pick up a few more things I need." Percival took his empty travel bags off his horse, throwing them over his shoulder.

"Mother is worried about you," said Bedivere, walking alongside Percival as he headed out of the stable and toward the kitchen. "So is Morag. My wife's sister and cousins should be arriving soon. They all want you here for Christmas."

"With all those people filling your great hall, no one is going to miss me."

"What's her name?" asked Bedivere, causing Percival to stop in his tracks and turn around.

"Pardon me?" he asked.

"You heard me. The girl. What's her name?" he asked with a silly grin.

Percival let out a deep sigh. There was no use lying to his brother. Bedivere was too observant and Percival could never hide anything from him.

"How did you know?" He turned and continued walking.

"Extra horse. No food. You being secretive. Come on, it's

written all over your face. Now tell me. Who is she and why can't she feed her own horse?"

"Because there is no food for animals or people at Imanie's cottage." Percival opened the door to the keep and headed inside.

"You're trying to woo a lady at that broken-down hovel?" Bedivere laughed. "Why don't you just bring her back here to the castle? Don't you think that might impress her more than a one-room cottage in the middle of the woods?"

"I asked her to come with me, but she didn't want to."

"So she stayed there by herself? Is that wise?"

They entered the kitchen. Percival plopped his travel bags down on one of the work tables. The servants were busy preparing food, having started before the light of day.

"She's not by herself. Her little brother is with her." Percival stretched his neck, looking around for food to pilfer. When he picked up a string of sausages and a loaf of bread, the head cook, an older plump woman, glared at him but didn't say a word since he was a noble and entitled to whatever he wanted.

"Bernice, have you any fruit tarts?" asked Percival, remembering how much Noel wanted tarts.

"Nay," griped the woman. "And I won't be making those until later. They are for the Christmas dinner, not to be given away," she scoffed.

"Never mind." He shoved some cheese and nuts into the bag next, followed by a handful of dried fruits. Carefully wrapping a few brown eggs in a cloth, he took those as well. Then he wandered over to a servant plucking the feathers off chickens. "This will do nicely." He picked up a whole, uncooked chicken, wrapping a towel around it, and topping off his bag.

"What are you doing?" asked Bedivere. "That isn't even cooked yet!"

"It doesn't matter. Holly is a damned good cook. It seems she can make something out of nothing so she'll do her magic to it."

"Holly, huh? So does this Holly have a surname?"

"Damn," mumbled Percival, grabbing a jug of ale and a bottle of wine and shoving corks into the necks before putting them under his arm. "You tricked me into telling you what you wanted to know."

"So, Lady Holly is from which castle? And how the hell is it that she's staying in a hovel with you? This is odd indeed. Spill your secrets, Brother."

"Bedivere, I don't need you asking so many questions. And I don't want you telling anyone that I've got a girl with me in the secret garden. Do you understand? No one is to know."

"Percival, you have a lassie in the secret garden?" Morag overheard, walking up to join them.

"Why me?" groaned Percival, wanting to rip his tongue out for being so careless. Morag, as lovely a girl as she was, also happened to be the biggest gossip in the castle. He never meant for her to hear any of this. Morag had tried to stop gossiping when she met Bedivere, but the girl was hopeless and still did it on occasion. One thing about Morag was that she always wanted to know everyone's business and she never stopped talking. The last thing he wanted was for her to know about his doings. She would tell everyone now.

"Morag, no matter what you thought you heard me say,

forget it. I didn't say it and it is none of your business." He hoped that would shut her up.

"Percival," said Bedivere in a warning voice. "Be nice. That is my wife and the lady of castle you are speaking to, remember."

Morag sucked in her cheeks, not saying a word. Then, she nodded slowly. "Husband, I will be gone for a short while. I am goin' ridin'."

"Not by yourself, you're not." Bedivere didn't like the idea in the least.

"Of course, no'. My cousin Maira just arrived. I'll take her with me."

"I still don't like the idea of two women out alone," protested Bedivere.

"Maira is as good with a sword as any man and ye ken it. We'll be safe."

"Take her husband's squire with you as well, or I won't agree to you leaving the castle at all."

"You want us to take Branton?" She raised a brow and her voice got higher. It was clear she didn't want him along. Branton had once been a page and grew up with Morag and her sister and cousins at Rothbury Castle, where they had been the wards of the late Lord Walter Beaufort. He had been their guardian until the day he died.

"Is there something wrong with taking Branton?" asked Bedivere.

"I dinna think we need him, that's all."

"Branton will go with you or you'll stay here," he told her.

"Fine. I'll take Branton with us," said Morag with a deep sigh, heading away.

"Be back soon before another storm kicks up," Bedivere called out.

"I will. Oh, Bedivere. Yer mother has been askin' if you found Percival yet. Ye two better stop in the ladies solar and talk with her to put her mind at ease that Percival is here."

"I'm not staying." Percival didn't want to stop to see his mother. If so, he'd be here for at least another hour. He was in a hurry to get back to Holly.

"Percival, I think Morag is right," agreed Bedivere. "You need to stop and talk to Mother. Don't make her upset at Christmastime. Besides, there is too much going on here and I don't want her asking me to go out and find you again. I really don't have the time to be doing that."

"All right, all right," said Percival, blowing air from his mouth. "But no matter what Mother says, it doesn't change things. I will not be here for the celebrations. I can't stay long. I need to gather a few nails and possibly a board to fix a broken stair at the cottage and be on my way. Oh, and where can I find a few good wax candles?"

"If you knew what was good for you, Percival, you'd bring that girl and her brother back here tomorrow for the Christmas feast," Bedivere told him. "That would make Mother more than happy."

"Mayhap not," he mumbled, throwing his bag over his shoulder and heading for the solar. He realized his mother wanted the best for all her children. But he wasn't sure she'd agree to him harboring a mysterious woman who seemed to be hiding something. Especially when the girl wasn't even a noble.

HOLLY FELT on edge while waiting for Percival to return to the cottage. If one of Lord Neville's guards showed up, she and Noel would have no chance to escape on foot. As nervous as she felt, she had to keep calm. If not, Noel would pick up on her uneasiness. She was all Noel had now. He counted on her for his needs and safety and she couldn't let him down. She had to remain strong because she didn't want her little brother to be scared.

"Why do you keep looking out the window?" asked Noel, sitting at the table playing with a wooden horse—the only toy he had been able to bring with them because they left so quickly.

"I thought I heard Percival returning. I am sure I heard hoofbeats but mayhap I am wrong." She was about to close the shutters to keep out the cold when she noticed the old garden gate opening. "Percival!" she cried, closing the shutters. She ran to the hooks on the wall, grabbing her cloak and donning it. "You stay here inside where it is warm," she told her brother. "I'm going out to meet Percival."

Honestly, she hoped to be alone with him in the barn again. She couldn't stop thinking about the kiss they shared and wanted to experience it again, as well as anything else that might transpire between them.

Closing the door behind her, she was about to descend the stairs when she stopped dead in her tracks. There were three cloaked and hooded people atop horses entering the garden. She'd been careless and was mistaken. It wasn't Percival at all.

She spun around to go back in and lock herself in the house, but before she could, she heard a woman call out.

"Hello, lassie! Hello, there, I say."

"What?" Holly turned back, knowing that if these were castle guards, they would never have a woman with them.

A man hopped off his horse, helping dismount the woman who had called out to her. Then, the third person swung down on their own and she could see it was another woman. They quickly headed toward the house.

"Welcome to Imanie's secret garden," said the same blonde woman who had called out to her. She carefully ascended the broken stairs with the second woman right behind her. The man tended to the horses. "I am Lady Morag and this is my cousin, Lady Maira."

"Hello," said the second woman, lowering her hood so Holly could see her. This woman looked to be about the same age as the other. Both of them seemed about Holly's age of twenty-one. "Let's go inside out of the cold."

Lady Maira pushed past her, entering the house. Lady Morag did the same. Holly had no choice but to follow. Her gut twisted. These were noblewomen. And nobles might know of her situation and turn her in to Lord Neville.

"Who is that man with the horses?" asked Holly, entering the house and closing the door behind them.

"That is Branton. My husband's squire," explained Maira, removing her cloak and hanging it on a hook. When she did so, Holly saw that she wore a sword strapped to her side.

"Oh!" she exclaimed, holding a hand to her mouth.

"Dinna let Maira's sword bother ye. She's had it ever since we were children," said Morag, removing her cloak and hanging it up as well. "Speaking of children, who is this?" Morag had a nice smile. She walked over to Noel. The little boy jumped up, leaving his toy horse on the table, and ran over and hid behind Holly.

"This is my little brother, Noel," Holly told them. "Won't you please sit down?"

"I'll stoke the fire," said Maira, walking to the hearth while Morag took a seat at the table.

"Why are ye here?" asked Morag bluntly.

"I came with my brother to visit my grandmother, but I discovered she has died." Holly pulled Noel in front of her and smoothed down his hair.

"Imanie was your grandmother?" asked Maira, stacking the logs on the hearth and poking them with the iron rod.

"Yes." Holly didn't say anything more.

"I'm sorry about yer grandmother, but didna ye ken what happened to her?" asked Morag. "It happened almost three years ago."

"Nay, I didn't know. My mother died recently and Imanie was our last relative. Noel and I came here to live with her. It was my mother's dying wish."

"I don't remember Imanie saying she had a granddaughter. Or even a child for that matter." Maira sounded suspicious as she stood up and brushed off her hands.

"Maira, Imanie was secretive, ye ken that," said Morag. She looked over at Holly and her eyes opened wide. "Ye have a heart pin, too!" Morag jumped up and rushed over to Holly. "So do we. See?" She pushed her hair aside and showed Holly the brooch. Holly was still wearing her cloak which the brooch was pinned to, while the ladies wore the brooches right on their gowns.

"You're a Follower of the Secret Hearts?" asked Maira curiously.

"Well... no. Not really." Holly didn't want to lie to the women. "Actually, it was my mother's brooch. She gave it to me on her deathbed."

"So yer mother was a member of the secret group then," said Morag with a nod.

"I suppose," said Holly. "I don't really know anything about this secret group. Could you tell me about it?"

"Sure, we can," said Morag.

"Morag, nay." Maira shook her head. "There is a reason it is secret."

"Percival told me the group no longer exists." Holly tried to pump them for information.

"Well, we all gave up bein' members when we got married," said Morag. "And Imanie and her sister died, so I suppose that's true."

"We didn't really know anyone else who was a follower," explained Maira.

"What did this group do?" asked Holly. Noel rushed over and snatched up his toy horse and bolted over to the bed.

"Let's just say it was a group of strong women who did things that made a difference in the world," Maira told her.

"And took no credit for it," added Morag.

"We really can't say more." Maira threw Morag another guarded look.

"I suppose it doesn't matter." Holly ran her hand over the pin and removed her cloak. "I wasn't chosen as a member so I don't really need to know more."

"Where are ye from?" asked Morag. "A neighboring castle?"

"She's not a lady." Maira looked her up and down. "I'd

say she's naught more than a peasant by the way she's dressed. Mayhap even a servant."

Holly's heart leapt into her throat. "Nay. I'm not noble," she admitted, wanting to crawl under the table. How was she going to explain to the women why she was still here? She prayed they wouldn't find out the truth.

Thankfully, the door opened before Holly had to explain anything else. Branton walked in with Percival.

"Morag! I should have known you'd be here meddling," snapped Percival. "Why couldn't you have stayed at the castle where you belong?"

"If I had, I never would have met yer friends," said Morag. "I mean, since ye werena willin' to tell me about them."

"Mayhap you'd better leave now." Percival was telling, not asking.

"But we just got here," said Maira.

"There is another storm coming. Branton, take them back to the castle anon," ordered Percival.

"Aye, my lord. I'll get the horses." Branton headed back out the door and Percival glared at Morag.

"All right. We're leavin'," sniffed Morag, getting her cloak and handing Maira's to her. "Holly, I'd like to invite ye and yer brother to the castle tomorrow for the start of Christmastide. We will have a festive dinner. There will be lots of food and drinks, and mummers will be there entertainin'. Plus, the minstrels will be playin' lots of music for dancin'."

"Thank you, but I don't think so," said Holly.

"Will they have fruit tarts?" asked Noel from the bed.

"Of course," said Morag, laughing. "My castle cook will be makin' three different kinds. What is yer favorite?"

"I like apple," said Noel, running over to Holly with his horse in his hand. "Can we go, Holly? Can we, please?"

"There will also be many children yer age there for ye to play with," Morag added.

"Oh, I would like that, Holly. Can we go? Pleeeeease?" Noel tugged at her cloak.

"Stop it, Noel." Holly couldn't say yes, as much as she wanted to. It was just too risky. "We need to let Ladies Morag and Maira leave so they can get back to the castle before the approaching storm."

"I'll walk them out," offered Percival, leaving the cottage with Morag and Maira. He wanted the ladies far away from Holly and to stop asking so many questions.

Once they were out of earshot of Holly hearing them, Maira spoke up.

"Percival, you need to distance yourself from this girl. I fear she is trouble."

"How can ye say that?" asked Morag. "Holly and her brother are lovely people. There is nothin' to fear."

"She's hiding something, I know she is," Maira told them. "No woman and child would be out here in the woods in the middle of winter, alone and unescorted. Even if she is just a peasant."

"She told us she was here to visit her grandmother," said Morag.

"If Imanie really was her grandmother, then why didn't Holly even know the woman is dead? Besides, Imanie never talked about her." Maira was always the suspicious one, while Morag was more trusting. "If you don't believe me, as soon as Fia gets here, we'll have her talk to Holly. Fia can tell when anyone is lying, just by seeing their body language."

"Nay. No' Fia," said Morag, always having hated living in her older sister's shadow. "I can tell Holly is a good person. Percival, I want ye to bring her and her brother to the castle tomorrow for the celebration. No one should be alone on Christmastide."

"She won't be alone. She'll be with me," said Percival.

"Don't be silly," said Morag. "Christmas in this hovel is like bein' abandoned. And ye should come home because you are goin' to break yer mother's heart."

"Don't worry about it," said Percival, just wanting everyone to leave. "And don't say a word about this to my mother. If she finds out, I'll know you are the gossip who told her."

Percival knew that would keep Morag silent. After her whole life of being a gossip, the girl didn't want to be called that anymore. No different than Bedivere not wanting to still be called an assassin.

CHAPTER SEVEN

B y the time Percival had finished fixing the broken stairs and tending to the horses, and came inside, the snow storm had started up again. Opening the door to the cottage, wind and snow blew in with him. He had logs stacked in his arms, balancing them so high that they threatened to fall over.

"Let me get the door for you." Holly ran over and closed it as Percival stacked the logs at the hearth.

"This fire is eating up the wood quickly. This is the last of it in the barn. I wish I had thought to bring some from Rothbury. My mother kept me there so long, I left without thinking."

"It's all right. We can go out and search for more wood tomorrow," said Holly, placing the chicken she'd cooked onto a plate on the table. She'd used the fire to cook it, as well as some cabbage and leeks. And finding some nuts and dried fruit in Percival's bag, she cooked them up with fresh apples again. "I wish I had flour. If so, I could have made something better."

"This is fine. It looks delicious." Percival removed his cloak, so hungry he would eat anything right now and not complain. He hurried over to the table. "Oh, I forgot to give you this." He detached a small pouch from his belt and handed it to her. She opened it and looked inside.

"Oh, my! Salt?" She dipped in a finger and tasted it and made a sound that sounded lusty to him.

"Let me try some." Noel held out his hand.

"Salt is precious and only used by the nobles," she told her brother, letting him taste a few grains. He made a face. "We will use this sparingly."

"I can't wait to eat. I'm starved." Percival pulled out a chair.

"Nay, you don't! Wash up first," Holly scolded.

"Wash?" He frowned. "We don't have any water."

"Yes, we do. Holly collected snow and melted it over the fire," said Noel, bringing his horse over to a basin filled with water to show him. He pretended to make his horse drink.

"Well, you are efficient." After washing, Percival sat down at the table, reaching out for the chicken.

Holly cleared her throat. He stopped.

"Now what?" asked Percival.

"Since it is Christmastime, I think we need to say a prayer, thanking God for our food. Don't you?"

"Oh. I suppose so."

Holly reached out and held his hand as well as her brother's. She nodded, silently telling Percival to hold her brother's hand too.

Percival wasn't good with children. He'd never prayed holding hands like this before, either. Still, he knew if he wanted to eat, he'd better go through with it. If not, there was no telling how many more things Holly would think of to keep him from the meal.

"All right. Give me your hand." Percival reached out and put his hand around the little boy's.

"Is Percival going to lead the prayer?" asked Noel, innocently, not even realizing how unsettling this was to him.

"Go ahead," said Holly with a nod.

Percival was about to protest, but just to get it over with, he opened his mouth and said the first thing that came out. "Thank you for this food, and I hope there will be a lot more because I'm not used to starving."

"I hardly think that is proper," said Holly, taking over for him. "Thank you, God, for giving us not just this food, but a roof over our heads, fire on the hearth, and... each other." She looked directly at Percival when she said the last part. Her eyes roamed down to his mouth and he knew she was thinking about the kiss they'd shared. He was too. His body started to heat up as his thoughts ran away with wondering how it would feel to bed this girl.

"Amen." Percival said, quickly releasing their hands and grabbing for his plate. He had to get his mind off of lustful thoughts. When his fingers grazed past her curves earlier, he wanted to squeeze her but refrained himself from doing so.

"Breast?" she asked, causing his head to jerk upward. He nearly fell from his chair.

"What?" he asked.

"Do you like breasts or thighs?" She pointed at the chicken.

Damn. For a minute he thought she had read his mind.

He enjoyed both when it came to a beautiful woman. "Oh, that. It doesn't matter." He slowly released a breath, embarrassed that he felt himself stirring beneath his belt. Thank goodness, she couldn't see it. He held out his plate and she gave him a breast and a thigh.

"We're making Christmas wreaths after dinner to hang on the door and put in the windows," said Noel. "Will you help us?"

"Nay," he grunted, scooping vegetables onto his plate. "I don't do things like that. I told you I don't like anything to do with Christmas."

"Why not?" asked Noel. He held up his plate, wanting Percival to scoop vegetables onto it. His eyes were big and round.

Percival never helped children in this manner. He didn't really want to do it, but decided it might make Holly happy, so he did. "Christmas is a horrible time. A time of death. I don't need to be reminded." He scooped food onto the boy's plate and then continued eating.

"His father died on Christmas," Holly explained to Noel in a soft voice.

"Oh," said Noel, using his fingers to pick up some cabbage. He pretended to feed some to his toy horse. "We always liked Christmas at home," said the boy. "Holly's birthday is on Christmas, and my birthday was a couple of days ago. I'm five now."

"Really?" Percival stopped chewing and looked over at Holly. Was he being insensitive since this was a special day for her, even if he hated it? "Why didn't you tell me?"

"It's nothing but just another day," she said, looking

down. He was sure she was pretending not to care even though she did. "Noel, use your spoon, not your fingers."

For a woman who wasn't a noble, she certainly had manners. He'd never seen anything like it.

"I can't feed Henry if I use a spoon," complained Noel.

"Henry?" asked Percival, pouring wine from the bottle into his cup.

"It's what he named his horse," explained Holly.

"Why did you name him Henry?" Percival was curious.

"That was the name of the nice man who came to see Mother," said the boy.

"What?" Percival looked over at Holly.

"It was a friend. From back home," was all Holly said.

"Henry misses Alba and Trevor." Noel looked as if he were about to cry.

"And who are they?" asked Percival, lifting the cup to his mouth. He saw Holly looking at him and realized he'd served himself but not her. He put down the cup and scooted it over to her and then took Noel's cup and poured some in.

"That's enough," Holly stopped him. "I usually mix Noel's wine with water. I'll melt some more snow." She started to get up, but Percival stopped her.

"Sit and eat," he told her. "The boy is five now and can handle a little wine." He poured some for himself next.

"Holly, can we go back home and get Henry's friends? They're going to be scared there all alone." Noel petted his toy horse as he spoke.

"Put your horse down and eat your food," Holly told him.

"I'll take you home to get them," offered Percival. "Where is your home? Is it far?" He hoped to find out more about these two and figured this was a good way to do it.

"This is our home now," said Holly. "Noel, you will get more toys eventually. You shouldn't fret over the past. Now, finish eating and drink your wine."

Percival thought Holly was being a little harsh with the child. He almost felt sorry for the little boy. He also didn't understand why Holly wouldn't tell him where her home was. Maira was correct in saying the woman was hiding something.

The day went fast and little Noel, tired from the wine, ended up going to bed very early. Percival never should have insisted the boy drink the wine without it being watered down first. But all the children at the castle drank wine and ale. Fresh water was hard to come by, and only babies drank cow's milk. Noel's head was down on the table, his eyes closed and his horse clutched in his little hand.

"I told you not to give him straight wine." Holly got up from the table. "Well, he'll be sleeping for the rest of the night. I need to get him into bed."

"I'll do it," offered Percival, feeling responsible for the boy's situation. He jumped up and picked up Noel and his horse, carefully laying him in bed and pulling the covers up around him. "He really likes his horse and was so disappointed that you said he couldn't go home to get the rest of his toys." He stared down at the boy sleeping, slowly reaching out to brush a lock of Noel's dark hair out of his eyes. Why hadn't he ever noticed before the innocence of a child sleeping? He had younger siblings, but never had they looked this sweet.

"This is our home now. He just needs to learn to let go of things that don't matter." Holly started collecting the dirty dishes, bringing them over to the wash basin to clean them.

"It matters to him," said Percival.

Holly's head snapped up. "Well, we can't always get what we want, can we? The sooner my brother realizes that, the better off he will be." She dumped the dishes into the water.

"Do you really believe that?" He picked up the wooden cups and followed her to the wash basin. "Don't you think since it is Christmas, the boy should have his toys? After all, what else does he have to look forward to?" He handed her the cups.

"I'm sorry. You're right," she said, her hands stilling. She looked like she was about to cry. "But we can't go back. We just can't."

"What is it you're afraid of, Holly? Tell me, please." He caressed the side of her face with his hand and she looked up at him with tear-filled eyes.

"You wouldn't understand," she said in a breathy whisper.

"Mayhap I would if you'd trust me enough to tell me your secrets." He kissed her then, and it felt good. Damned good. Her lips were so soft and she tasted sweet from the wine and currants. And for some reason he thought she smelled like flowers. Mayhap it was just his longing for her that made him feel this way, but he needed her close to him. He pulled her into his arms and hugged her. She rested her head against his chest and he could feel the wetness of her tears right through his tunic.

"I'm sorry you have gotten involved in my problems, Percival. Mayhap it would be best if you just forgot about us and went back to the castle tomorrow. You have family there. They want you there. You need them."

"What I need is for you to trust me. I'm here for you, yet you keep shutting me out." He pulled her over to a chair and sat her atop his lap. "Now tell me, Holly. Where was your home and why can't you go back?"

"It doesn't matter." She wasn't giving him any information at all.

"It matters to me."

"Why do you hate Christmas so much?" She turned the question on him now.

"I told you. My father died on Christmas."

"Yes, you said that, but you didn't tell me why."

"If you must know, he died by hanging a few years ago. It was Christmastime. His abductors mocked him and decorated the gallows with holly and juniper boughs."

"Oh, my." She pulled away and sniffled. "I'm so sorry. I can see now why you don't like the holiday. Still, don't let your hatred for what happened to your father ruin all the good things about Christmas."

"I'll just be happy when the blasted holiday is over."

"Why was he hanged?"

This was a question he was hoping she wouldn't ask. But now, he was going to have to answer.

"I'll tell you, but only if you promise to tell me where you lived and why you really left. And why you cannot go back."

"That's three things you want to know from me, when I only asked one from you."

"Then at least give me one. That should be fair."

"All right," she said with a small nod. "You first."

He half-thought she was tricking him and wouldn't give him any information. But if he acted like he didn't trust her, she really wouldn't tell him a thing.

"My father was accused of plotting to kill the king."

"Oh!" Her eyes opened wide. "And was he really plotting to kill the king? Did you know about it?"

"That's two more questions. Are you willing to answer three for me?"

She slowly shook her head and he thought it was over. "Keswick," she told him.

"You lived in Keswick?" He'd heard of that town which wasn't far away, but had never really been there.

"Yes," she said, getting off his lap and saying nothing more. "Now, if you'll excuse me, I need to finish cleaning the dishes."

"Tomorrow is the start of Christmastide," he said, speaking of the eve before Christmas day. The celebrations would last for twelve days. He looked back at the boy. "Noel is going to be so upset that he didn't get to make wreaths before he fell asleep. He seemed so excited about it."

"Mayhap we can make them tomorrow."

Percival looked over at the remaining logs on the hearth. "Holly, there is only enough wood to make it through the night, if at that. If we're going to cook anything tomorrow, or want heat, we'll have to go out first thing to collect wood."

"We will," she said, seeming suddenly sad.

After putting a few more logs on the fire, he picked up a broken log, having an idea. He sat down on a chair and pulled out his knife, resting his feet on the table.

"What are you doing?" she asked, looking over her shoulder, still washing the dishes.

"I figure if Henry misses his friends, then I'll just have to carve him a new one." He started to whittle.

"You know how to do that?" she asked, sounding surprised.

"I can't say I've ever made a child's toy before, but how hard can it be?"

Well, he found out exactly how hard it was, three hours later when he still didn't have anything that remotely resembled a farm animal.

"I'm going to bed," Holly announced with a yawn. He looked up to see her standing in her shift, holding a blanket in front of her. "Where will you sleep?"

"How big is that bed?" he asked, really wanting to share it with her.

"It wouldn't be proper for you to sleep with me and my brother."

"And neither is it proper to be wasting all our wood to end up with something like this." He held up the toy he had been trying to carve.

"What's that?" she asked, peering through the dark to see it. The room was only lit by the one taper candle that had almost burned down to a stub already.

"It's Henrietta. Henry's friend." He held it up to show her.

"Is that supposed to be a... frog?"

"Nay," he said, frowning. "It's a pig. Can't you tell?"

She giggled and climbed under the covers. "I'm sure Noel will love it. Good night."

Percival turned the blob of wood one way and then another, but as hard as he tried, he really couldn't think of this as a pig. He yawned, being very tired. Putting down his knife, he leaned his head back on the chair and once again rested his feet on the table. Damn, what he would give to be in a nice soft, warm bed right now instead of on a cold, hard chair in the midst of an almost-dead fire.

Tomorrow, things were going to change, he decided. Because if they were all going to be living here, then he had every right to sleep in the same damned bed.

CHAPTER EIGHT

"Holly, wake up! Holly, look!" Noel tugged at Holly's sleeve, waking her from her wonderful dream of being intimate with Percival.

"Go back to sleep, Noel." She turned over, hugging the pillow, not wanting to be disturbed.

"Look what's on the table. How did that get there?" Her brother's voice was so excited, that it made Holly curious. The only thing on the table last night when she went to sleep was Percival's feet.

"All right, let me see." She sat up and yawned, stretching her arms over her head. It seemed so warm in here that she thought she was dreaming. Didn't Percival say they only had enough firewood to make it through the night? Rubbing her eyes, she swung her feet to the floor as Noel darted across the room and climbed atop a chair.

"Look, Henry. You have new friends," she heard the little boy say, thunking his toy horse across the table, making it run.

"Oh. It's a pig," said Holly, making her way to the table. She wanted Noel to know what kind of animal it was supposed to be so he didn't disappoint Percival by asking. Where was Percival anyway? She looked around the room for him and that is when she noticed something that hadn't been there last night.

The fire burned hot. A large pile of logs was next to the hearth. And to her surprise, there were juniper boughs on the table, and acorn, and even sprigs of holly and what she thought might be mistletoe. They were arranged around a big red wax candle in the center. If she wasn't mistaken, she even smelled cinnamon.

The door to the cottage opened, and Percival walked in yawning, carrying a wreath and fussing with it as he entered.

"Percival. There you are," said Holly.

He stopped in his tracks. "Oh, you're up. I wanted to hang this on the door before you awoke but it took me longer than I thought to shape the half-frozen grapevines into a circle and weave the branches from the greens through it." He held it up for them to see. "Did I do it right? This is the first time I ever attempted anything like this."

"It's beautiful," said Holly, walking over to take it from him. It was lopsided and needed a lot more greenery but it was special to her since he made it. "I thought you said you don't like decorations or anything having to do with Christmas."

"I still don't," he said, closing the door. "But I know you two like those kinds of things."

"Well, thank you. That was very thoughtful. You must have gotten up pretty early to collect all that firewood and even put together a nice table for the holiday."

"And I was hungry so I cooked up some eggs and sausage

if you two are hungry." He opened the top of an iron pot near the hearth and showed her. "I used salt and everything."

"Oh, my that is a surprise. How did you get all this done this morning?"

"Actually, I didn't sleep at all."

"Oh, Percival, nay." She wasn't using his title and he didn't seem to care. Holly liked it better this way.

"Look, Percival, look!" Noel ran over with his hands full and Holly stretched her neck to see what all he had. "Henry the horse has new friends. This is Beauregard the Bear and Walter the Wolf. Now Henry won't be lonely."

"I think that's a pig, sweetheart," Holly told him.

"Uh, uh," said Percival shaking his head. "It's a bear. Just like the boy said."

"Percival carved those for you, Noel."

"Thank you!" Noel wrapped his arms around Percival's legs and gave him a big squeeze before running back to the bed to play with his new toys.

"What happened to Henrietta the Pig?" whispered Holly.

Percival spoke from behind his hand. "If the boy thinks it's a bear then that is just what we'll call it. As long as he is happy he can call it any animal he likes."

Holly giggled.

"Oh, Noel, I made something else that will be fun for all of us." Percival pulled something out of his pocket. He walked over to the table and spun it. Noel rushed over to see it.

"It's a top," said Holly. "How clever."

Percival leaned over and whispered. "It's what was left of Duncan the Duck that didn't turn out either." They both laughed at that. Noel squealed with delight. It did Holly's heart good to see her little brother smiling instead of being sad at Christmas. After all the hardships they'd been through lately, especially with the deaths of their mother and grandmother, they really needed something good to transpire in their lives. And thanks to Percival, that had just happened.

"Thank you," she said, getting on her tip-toes and kissing him quickly on the lips. He had a silly look on his face when she walked across the room with the wreath. "I'll hang the wreath on the door."

"This is the best Christmas ever," shouted little Noel. "And now, I'll have lots of toys to play with once I meet all the children at the castle."

"What?" Holly spun around so fast that she almost dropped the wreath.

"Percival said we could go to his castle for fruit tarts on Christmastide and that means today. Yay!" shouted the little boy, running around the room with his new toys in his hands, holding them high in the air.

"Noel, we're not going to—"

"Shhh," said Percival, holding his finger to her lips. "You don't want to spoil the boy's good mood, do you?"

"What are you saying?"

"I'm saying, you two better hurry and dress because those fruit tarts go fast and we don't want to miss them."

"Nay, Percival, we can't go to the castle. I'm sorry but you'll have to go without us."

"Of course, you can go. You've been invited not only by me, but also by Lady Morag. How can you turn us both down?" asked Percival.

"But I—"

"No more excuses, my sweet Holly." He must have been addled from his lack of sleep because he pulled her into his arms and kissed her deeply and passionately right there in front of her brother. Noel was playing with his new toys and thankfully didn't seem to notice. "Now get dressed and be sure to douse the flames on the hearth. I'll be out in the barn readying the horses for our trip."

He didn't give her time to object. He turned and opened the door while she stood there with her mouth wide open.

"Oh, and I already have a nail on the door to hang this on." He plucked the wreath from her hands and slapped it atop the nail on the outside of the door, yawning once again, admiring his work. "Mayhap, if I feel up to it later, I might even try making one of those silly kissing balls that Morag likes so much. Then again, who needs one of them to kiss a pretty woman?"

Before she knew what was happening, she was pulled into his arms again, her lips locked with his. A warmth traveled through her body. Something inside her stirred to life being in Percival's embrace. She wanted more than anything to spend Christmas with him at the castle with his family. Plus, it would be so nice to see Noel playing with other children. Not to mention, she was looking forward to a fruit tart as well. She hugged her arms around her and leaned her head against the door next to the wreath, watching Percival take the stairs two at a time, hurrying to the barn to get the horses.

Little snowflakes fell all around her, and she swore she could hear her grandmother's voice telling her that she could do anything and not to be afraid.

"Mayhap we will go to the castle for Christmas," she said aloud, feeling hope fill her. There would be a lot of people there, so mayhap no one would know who she and Noel were. They could just disappear into the crowd and no one would know better. Mayhap, just mayhap, this would be the best Christmas ever, just like Noel said.

———

WITHIN THE HOUR, Percival, Holly, and Noel arrived at Rothbury Castle. This time, Percival wasn't regretting Christmas at all. Oddly enough, he was rather looking forward to the celebration. It was because he wanted to make sure Holly and Noel had a good time. Sure, he was so tired one could knock him over with a feather, but it was all worth it. Just seeing the pleased look on Holly's face this morning and hearing the squeals of joy from Noel made giving up his sleep worth it.

Was this what Holly was talking about when she told him Christmas was important to her family? He'd lost sight of this over the years, but now he was remembering that it used to be important to him growing up as well. It was because he, his parents, and his siblings were all together. They were a family.

Percival felt good about the way he was changing. Holly and Noel seemed to fill an empty spot inside him. A spot that he'd guarded and not let anyone fill because of his anger toward the people who had killed his father on Christmas. Perhaps he had only been making himself miserable by holding on to these demons of the past. Bedivere was right. He needed to replace his bad memories with good ones, and he was starting that right now.

He never felt better. He'd managed to make a little boy

happy and a beautiful woman trust him enough to let him take her into his world... even though she still hadn't shared hers with him.

It didn't matter, he decided. No matter what secrets Holly was keeping, right now he didn't even care. All that mattered was that he was making them, as well as himself, happy. Mayhap this had something to do with the spirit of Christmas that Holly spoke of. Because of Holly, he realized he was wrong about hating Christmas. This year would be different. He would forget all the bad memories and make new, happy ones with Holly and Noel at his side. Yes, this Christmas was going to change everything for him.

"All right, we're here," he told Noel who was riding with him. "Now, hold on to your toys and don't lose them. It took too damned long to make them and I don't think I have it in me to try again."

He dismounted and helped the little boy off the horse.

"This castle is bigger than Lord Neville's," said Noel, looking around with wide eyes.

"Lord Neville?" asked Percival, finally getting some information about where they came from. Still, he needed more.

"Noel, stop talking so much and stay close to me." Unfortunately, Holly had already dismounted and was right behind them, silencing the boy when Percival was finally going to get some answers.

HOLLY GRABBED her brother's arm, not wanting him talking about Lord Neville, because some of the nobles, or mayhap all of them, were sure to know who he was. She didn't need or want trouble today. She was hoping to get lost in the crowd and join in with the celebrations without anyone noticing them.

Taking a minute to look around, Holly felt in awe by all that she saw.

The courtyard bustled with servants, merchants, alewives, tradesmen, and nobles. Serving girls brought ale and spiced wine to the occupants, while children ran in circles chasing a dog. The merchants were selling their wares today, ranging from fresh fish to shoes to even fancy head-pieces made for the noblewomen. Everyone seemed to be there, even the villagers, townsfolk, and those who looked like serfs, just like herself. Lord Bedivere seemed to want to include everyone in the Christmas celebrations. He even gave the people a chance to sell their wares and make money for their family. Lord Bedivere seemed to be a good, fair man.

Holly admired that. Lord Neville never invited a serf into his courtyard unless they were delivering crops they grew for him. And instead of allowing the people to make money, he just kept raising his taxes, demanding more money from them instead.

Percival picked up a wreath from a table, inspecting it and making a face. "Ah. I see what I did wrong now. I needed more greens. And if I used smaller grapevines, I would have been able to bend them easier."

"Would you like to buy a wreath for your lady?" asked the peasant from behind the table.

"My lady?" He looked up in surprise, and then glanced at Holly. "Oh, he means you," he said.

Holly blushed. Surely, just by seeing her simple clothes the man must have realized she wasn't a noble. She felt embarrassed by this, because she wished she was a lady. Percival's lady. Which she wasn't and neither could she ever be.

"Nay, nay," said Percival shaking his head and putting the wreath back on the table. "I know how to make these myself now, so I don't need to spend coin on buying them." He took Holly by the arm and led her away, with Noel following. "Holly, I think I can improve the wreath I made. I know what I did wrong now just by looking at the vendor's wreaths. I'll fix it up later and it'll be better, I promise."

"I was fine with the one you already gave me," said Holly, smiling and holding on to his arm. It was refreshing to see a lord take such interest in something that usually only peasants, servants, and women did. He was doing it all for her. She was sure of it. His actions touched her heart.

"Percival! Holly! Ye came." Lady Morag pushed through the crowd with two noblewomen right behind her. "And Noel is here too. Oh, good. I am so happy you decided to join us for Christmastide."

"Lady Morag," said Percival, not sounding happy to see her.

"Who is this, Morag?" asked one of the women with long, red hair.

"Och, silly of me no' to tell ye. Fia, this is Holly and Noel. They are Percival's friends. Holly and Noel, this is my sister, Lady Fia, and my cousin, Lady Willow," she told them pointing to each of the women in turn. The one named Fia wore a Highland plaid of purple, blue and green. Morag's cousin, Willow was a vision of beauty. Her long, dark hair was pulled up and her head encircled with a jeweled headpiece. Her gown was burgundy velvet, etched with lots of lace. Just being in their presence made Holly feel so out of place. Still, she was happy to meet them.

"Are you here for the Christmas celebration and festivities?" asked the dark-haired woman named Willow.

"Yes. Yes, we are," said Holly.

"I dinna remember hearin' about ye. Where did ye and Percival meet?" asked Fia, the Scottish sister of Morag.

This took her by surprise and she didn't know how to answer.

"Holly is the granddaughter of Imanie," Percival broke in. "She came to stay with her for the holidays but didn't know of Imanie's passing."

"Oh. I'm so sorry," said Fia, eyeing up the heart pin. "I see you have a heart brooch."

"It was my mother's." Holly's finger covered the brooch and she fingered it nervously. "She gave it to me on her deathbed a few days ago."

"Blethers, this is all so depressin'," said Morag.

Holly needed to change the subject quickly. When Fia opened her cloak, Holly saw the big bump of her stomach.

"Oh, are you pregnant, Fia?" asked Holly.

"Aye," she answered.

"She's not usually that fat," said Percival with a chuckle, getting a nasty glare from each of the girls.

"I am due any day now," said Fia, rubbing her belly and smiling. "This is my second child."

"Congratulations," Holly told her.

"My sister was born on Christmas and that is why our mother named her Holly," said Noel. "My birthday was a few days ago."

"Well, how nice," said Fia. "Mayhap my bairn will be born on Christmas too. I'd like that."

"I'm sure Bedivere wouldn't." Percival spoke up again. "He won't want anything ruining the Christmastide celebrations."

"Percival!" said Holly in shock. "That would add to the happiness, not ruin a thing."

"You address him without using his title?" Willow looked at her from the corners of her eyes.

"I-I..." Once again, Holly was caught off-guard and didn't know what to say. She needed to be more careful.

"I told her it was all right." Percival reached out and put his arm around her shoulders.

"I'm sorry. I didn't mean to be disrespectful," apologized Holly with a bow of her head. "I've just not been thinking straight since the death of my mother and discovering my grandmother is gone as well."

"Why dinna ye join us with celebratin' Christmastide?" suggested Morag. "That will certainly cheer ye up."

"Where are the children you told me about?" asked Noel, poking his head out from behind Holly. "I have new toys I want to show them." He held out his wooden toys that Percival carved for him.

"Well, my daughter, Oletha, is quite a bit younger than ye," said Fia, placing her hands on her pregnant belly and smiling at the boy. "And ye'll have to wait for a while yet if you want to play with the new baby."

"My daughter Siusan is too young to play with you, and so is our cousin's daughter, Sable," said Willow.

"My daughter Mazelina is still just a baby," said Morag. "I don't think any of them will make good playmates for ye."

"Aren't there any boys at this castle?" Noel crinkled his nose in disgust.

"Percival, you said you had young brothers, didn't you?" asked Holly.

"Yes, I do." Percival yawned before continuing. "I'm sure Luther and Avery would love to see your new toys, Noel. I just have to find them first."

"I ken exactly where they are. Would ye like me to take ye to them?" asked Fia, holding out her hand.

"Yes!" Noel shoved all his toys into the fold of his arm and held out his hand for Fia.

"I'll go with you," said Holly, not wanting to leave her brother alone with strangers.

"Nay, you won't," said Willow. "You'll want to look good if you are going to be hanging on to Lord Percival's arm. In that gown, you will just be the brunt of the morrow's gossip." She shook her head, looking Holly up and down in disgust.

"But this is the only gown I have. I mean... the only one that I brought with me." She didn't want them to know she was naught but a poor serf instead of a merchant's daughter with only one gown to her name.

"That's not a problem. I brought several extra gowns with me," said Willow. "I always travel with lots of extra clothes because you never know when you might need them. I'll let you borrow one if you'd like. After all, you'll want to look pretty when you're kissing Percival under the kissing bough." She giggled and so did Morag.

When Percival didn't respond, Holly looked over at him to see him standing there with his eyes closed. She swore he was sleeping.

"Percival?" She shook his arm and he jerked, his eyes popping open.

"What is it? What's wrong?" he blurted out, his hand going to the hilt of his sword.

Morag and Willow giggled more.

"We are stealin' yer lover to dress her up for the celebration." Morag grabbed onto Holly's arm and pulled her closer.

"Lover? Oh, nay, you're mistaken. We just met. We're not lovers," said Holly, looking back at Percival who just smiled and shrugged, not saying a word to deny it at all.

"Well, with that ugly gown, of course not. I can see why you are not lovers," said Willow taking her by her other arm. "Men like women who are pretty."

"Willow, how can ye say she is no' pretty? I think she is very pretty indeed," said Morag.

"That's not what I meant." Willow tried to correct herself. "I was talking about her clothes only. Face it. This gown is plain and drab and ugly." Willow reached out to touch Holly's gown, but then pulled back her hand before she did so. "It doesn't matter. I can fix that. Come on, we don't have too much time and lots to do to ready you for the celebration. The meal is about to start so we need to work fast."

"Well I-I don't know. I don't think I should wear the gown of a noble. It's not proper since I am only a commoner." Holly looked back at Percival as the women pulled her away.

"Go on with them," said Percival with a wave of his hand. "I can't win an argument with Lady Morag or Lady Willow, so why bother trying? If they want to dress you up, then let them."

"I-I'll see you soon," said Holly, being whisked through the crowd by the other women.

Percival heard a deep chuckle and turned to see Bedivere standing there with his arms crossed over his chest. His eyes were fastened to Holly.

"So, I see you really did find yourself a girl to bed after all," said his brother. "I can also tell it has already helped your sour disposition. You don't seem nearly as grouchy as before."

"Nay, you're wrong. I haven't bedded her," said Percival. "And I wish you wouldn't talk that way about Holly. She is sweet and doesn't deserve to be treated as if she were a whore."

"So, is she?"

"What?" Percival felt his anger growing. "What the hell does that mean?"

"All I'm saying is, what do you really know about the girl? I mean, what can you tell me?"

"Well, I know she comes from the town of Kestwick," said Percival.

"Really. Is she a lady then? From Castle Kestwick mayhap?"

"Nay, she's not noble. She said she wasn't. I believe she lives in town."

"Why is she traveling alone with the boy?"

"I don't know. Mayhap she likes to travel alone. I didn't ask her."

"It's odd she doesn't have a male escort. Dangerous too. Isn't she married?"

"I don't know, and I wish you wouldn't ask me things like that." This thought upset Percival deeply. He never even considered that Holly might already be married. Why hadn't he thought to ask?

"You really don't know anything else about her, do you?"

"She doesn't talk about herself much."

"Then, she's hiding something. Something that she doesn't want you to know."

"That's not true!" Percival had considered the same thought, but dismissed it. He didn't want to think of Holly as someone who might be hiding a tarnished past. "Some things just don't need to be talked about. I mean, why does it even matter?"

"Why does it matter, you ask? And what do you mean *it doesn't need to be talked about*? You make no sense." They walked together toward the great hall.

"What I'm saying is that I never told her I spent time in prison along with the rest of my family or that you were an assassin. I didn't feel it was necessary to bring it up, so I didn't mention it."

"I appreciate you not bringing up my past, Percival. But don't you think you should at least mention that you were in prison before she hears it from someone else?"

"I can't really do that without telling her the whole story, now can I? Which means I would have to bring up you, Brother."

"I see. I suppose you have a point there."

Percival couldn't stop yawning.

"For a man who didn't bed the wench, you certainly seem as if you didn't get much sleep at all."

"I didn't." One more yawn. "I was up all night carving toys out of wood for Noel and making wreaths and... Christmas type things."

"You what?" Bedivere stopped in his tracks and burst out laughing. "What happened to hating anything to do with Christmas, and thinking tending to children makes you less of a man?"

"You were the one who told me to make new Christmas memories, so that is what I did. Now, shut up about all this. You're making my head hurt. Let's go get some whisky."

"I think the wench changed you, and I can't say I'm disappointed. Now, I might just know where we can get some of the best whisky in all England and Scotland."

"Are you talking about the MacKeefe's Mountain Magic?"

"Aye. Reed brought some with him from Scotland when he arrived with his family. Let's go find it."

Reed was one of the Legendary Bastards of the Crown and also the father of Fia and Morag. He, and his brothers, Rowen and Rook, were triplets.

"Mountain Magic it is, then," said Percival with one more big, long yawn.

"You'd better stop that and close your mouth before you start attracting flies," Bedivere told him, laughing as he said it.

The only thing Percival wanted to attract was Holly. And hopefully after a little of the famous Mountain Magic, he'd even work up enough nerve to kiss her under one of those stupid kissing boughs in front of everyone.

CHAPTER NINE

"Oh, my, this is beautiful," exclaimed Holly, holding out her arms, looking at herself in the standing mirror.

"Of course, it is. It's one of my gowns and all my clothes are the finest you'll ever see," said Willow. "I'm known for wearing nice things."

"Willow, ye are comin' across as haughty again," Morag told her with a scowl.

"Sorry. I didn't mean anything by that," said Willow.

"Are you sure I should really wear this?" Holly couldn't take her eyes of her reflection. It was as if she were dreaming. She looked like a princess. Someone like her should never be wearing anything like this. It was wrong. Really wrong. "I mean... this is the gown of a lady."

"Of course, ye should wear it," Morag told her, fussing with Holly's long sleeve that covered her knuckles and hung all the way down to the floor. It is Christmastime. And today ye'll feel like a lady even if you're only a townsfolk."

"What town are you from and what do your parents do?" asked Willow, brushing Holly's hair with a boar bristle brush.

"I come from... Kestwick," she told them. "My mother was a midwife."

"Kestwick? That's not far from here," said Willow. "I believe my husband knows the lord of the castle."

"Oh. Does he," said Morag, not offering Lord Neville's name.

"What kind of work does your father do?" Willow continued.

"My father is dead, as well as my mother," she told them, suddenly feeling as if this conversation was going in a direction she didn't want it to go. "So, you're going to braid my hair?" she asked, changing the conversation. "Will it be wrapped up atop my head as well?"

"Yes, we're braiding it and it'll be adorned with holly, just like your name," said Willow, putting down the boar's-bristle brush. "You never told us what kind of work your father did."

The girl wasn't going to drop the subject. And she didn't seem like the kind of woman who liked her questions ignored. Holly realized she was going to have to give her some kind of an answer.

"We have a... a farm," she told him, which wasn't a lie. She just didn't relay the information that she was forced to farm the land for Lord Neville as well as pay lots of rent to the evil man.

"A farm?" Willow almost seemed stunned. "You don't act like a farmer, or speak like one either. I would have guessed you were the daughter of a merchant."

"My father liked farming," she said, barely remembering her father since he died when she was young. "My mother actually worked for the nobles as well as the townsfolk. She was one of the best midwives in the land."

Just when Willow was about to ask another question, there thankfully came a knock on the bedchamber door. Then Fia poked her head inside the room.

"The meal is startin' and the children are already in the great hall," announced Fia. "We need to hurry. Father willna like us bein' late."

"Och, she's right," said Morag, fastening a piece of holly into Holly's hair. "Our da likes to eat and doesna like to wait when there is food present."

"Yes, we should go," said Holly, breathing out a sigh of relief. This couldn't have come at a better time. Hopefully, she'd be able to avoid any more questions for the rest of the day.

"Wait!" said Willow with a halting hand in the air.

Holly cringed and turned back toward the girl. Mayhap she wouldn't be so lucky after all.

"You don't want to forget your mother's brooch. This is very important." Willow held it up in the air.

"Yes. Yes, it is," said Holly as Willow pinned it onto Holly's bodice. "Although, I'm not sure I should be wearing that either. I mean, I am not a member of the Followers of the Secret Heart."

"If yer mother gave it to ye on her deathbed, she must have done so for a reason," said Morag. "I wasn't a member either, but Imanie gave me her pin and let me join the group."

"Oh," said Holly, now knowing what happened to her grandmother's heart brooch and why she hadn't found it at the cottage. In a way, Holly envied Morag, because it sounded as if mayhap she'd spent more time with Holly's grandmother than she ever did.

"Aye," agreed Willow. "I'm sure your mother saw you as a strong woman, and this heart brooch proves it." She clasped the brooch and tapped it with her finger. "Mayhap, you'll do something to make a difference in the world, like the rest of us," Willow added.

Holly sincerely doubted that. After all, what difference could a common serf make with anything? She really wondered about her mother and what the woman had done as a member of this special group. No matter what it was, it no longer mattered since both her mother and grandmother were gone from this world for good. The only difference Holly could make was to change her life and the future for her brother by staying hidden for a year and a day. But that was never going to happen if these women kept asking her so many questions.

WHEN HOLLY WALKED out into the great hall with Willow and Morag, Percival couldn't believe his eyes. Holly looked so beautiful! Anyone would swear she was a lady. He put down his tankard and pushed the wooden spinning top over to Noel and his brothers, running over to escort her into the room.

Wearing one of Willow's ornate gowns, Holly was dressed in bright green with white lace. The long tippets, or sleeves, reached all the way down to the soft, pointy satin slippers on her feet. Her hair was braided, and in the braid were woven sprigs of dark green holly with bright red berries.

Her clear blue eyes sought him out. She looked frightened and he didn't want her to feel this way. He smiled at her and winked. The fear in her gaze seemed to leave her, once she saw his face.

"My, you are beautiful," he told her, holding out his arm. May I escort you to the table?"

"Yes. Please," she said, being ever so polite, taking his arm, gripping him tightly with her fingers.

"Mmmph," he mumbled as he headed toward the dais where the nobles sat. "Any tighter with that grip and you're going to draw blood."

She leaned over and spoke softly. "Percival, everyone is staring at me. I'm so nervous that I feel my body shaking."

"Of course, they are all staring, and rightly so," he said, still heading for the dais. "You are the most beautiful woman in the entire room."

"Nay, don't say that. You know it is not true."

"It is true to me." He reached out and stroked her cheek, looking deeply into her eyes, feeling his body warming just being in her presence."

"Thank you," she said in a mere whisper. When he continued to walk toward the dais, she suddenly stopped in place. "Don't take me up there, please. I cannot go. It is not right."

"Why not?" he asked.

"You know as well as I that the commoners eat below the salt. Only the nobles sit at the dais."

"I really don't think anyone would object. I mean, you look like a lady today, even if you aren't one. Besides, you are my guest, and that is where I am going to sit since I am brother to the lord of the castle."

"Please, Percival, don't make me do this," she begged. Her voice quaked and her face paled. He wasn't sure she wouldn't swoon. She gripped his arm even tighter, and he could feel her entire body trembling. He realized she really didn't want to go up the stairs, even though he wanted more than anything to bring her with him. Not wanting to make her feel more uncomfortable than she already was, he decided it best to just sit below the salt with her.

"Fine. We'll sit by Noel and my brothers. I want to keep an eye on those toys since they were so hard to make and took so long."

"But you shouldn't sit below the salt. Your place is on the dais, Percival."

"My place is with you today, Holly. And if you are sitting below the salt, then so am I."

"Thank you," she said, reaching up and giving him a quick peck on the cheek.

"Ye'll have to do better than that since ye're standin' under the kissin' bough," called out Morag from her seat at the dais.

"What?" Percival looked up at the ceiling and groaned. Sure enough, one of those silly kissing boughs was directly over their heads where they stood. "We don't have to do this," he told her, not wanting to terrorize her more with everyone watching. Actually, he wasn't feeling all that confident about kissing her in front of everyone either. Although, with the way she looked, he wanted to kiss her more than anything right now.

"Of course, not. We won't kiss." Her long lashes lowered and she stared at the floor. "It would be silly."

If he didn't know better, he'd think she was a bit disappointed. It was almost as if she wanted to kiss him under the blasted thing. A minute ago she was too upset to go up to the dais, but now she wanted to kiss in front of all the nobles? He really didn't understand this girl at all.

"Brother, take a seat," called out Bedivere. "Father John is going to lead us in a prayer so we can eat."

"Sorry," said Percival, escorting Holly to the table with the children, taking a seat across from her on the long wooden bench. The prayer was said and the food and drinks served. This opened the feast and the start of the Christmastide celebration.

HOLLY HAD NEVER TASTED SUCH a delicious meal in her entire life. Percival kept apologizing that the food wasn't as good as up at the dais, but it was still better than anything she'd ever eaten in her life.

The feast started with a rich, thick soup that actually had meat in it, along with lots of vegetables, spices, and even salt! That was followed by pickled rabbit in a dill gravy. Boar's head with brawn pudding was part of the meal, as well as roasted goose with sugared quince and lots of walnuts and currants. Root vegetables were served alongside a thick cut of venison drenched in brown gravy that Percival brought to her from up at the dais. He insisted he wanted her to taste it, but honestly she thought it was only because he personally didn't want to miss out. The highlight of the meal and the star piece was a cooked peacock in full display with its feathers reattached and spread out in a beautiful array of colors.

"Oh, my! This is all so amazing," she exclaimed. "I've

eaten more today than I can ever remember. I am so full I couldn't eat another bite," she told Percival near the end of the meal. He kept filling her goblet with red mulled wine, so her head was already spinning. He was drinking some kind of strong whisky that she could smell all the way across the table. He offered some to her but she declined, already starting to feel giddy.

"Where are the fruit tarts?" asked Noel, getting to his knees on the bench and leaning on the table to talk to Percival. "I thought you said there would be fruit tarts but I don't see any." He pouted.

"Just be patient," he told the boy. "They are coming right now, along with the mince pie and seed cake." Noel's pout turned into a smile when the servers came with the sweets.

"I want one of each flavor," shouted Noel, standing up on the bench now and grabbing for one off the full tray that the server placed on the table.

"Noel, sit down before you fall." Holly pulled him back down to a sitting position. Everyone started grabbing for the tarts and the boy wasn't able to reach them. He looked up with wide eyes, looking like he was about to cry.

"Hold it!" Percival got up and scooped up two handfuls of tarts in flavors of cherry, apple, plum, and pear. He brought them over and put them down in front of Noel. "All right, continue," he said sitting back down. Noel's eyes opened wide as he dug his spoon into one after another, wanting to taste each one.

The musicians started playing music while some of the trestle tables at the other end of the hall were dismantled to make more room to dance.

"Noel will be busy for a while," Percival told Holly. "Would you care to dance?"

"Dance?" Her head snapped up and that frightened look was back on her face again. "Me?"

Percival laughed. "Of course, *you*. Whom do you think I am talking to?"

"Well, I... don't know."

HOLLY'S HEART skipped a beat when Percival asked her to dance. She wanted to dance, but wasn't even sure how. Or at least she didn't know how the nobles did it. Plus, it probably wasn't a good idea. She didn't belong on the dance floor. Serfs never danced alongside nobles. There was really no reason for her to be there unless she was clearing away the trenchers or perhaps serving wine.

"You don't know?" Percival looked at her and grinned. He was getting relaxed from all the whisky and she noticed the look of lust in his eyes. She liked it, actually. He was so handsome and so kind that she couldn't stop staring. "Of course, you would, Holly," he continued. "It's Christmas."

Percival seemed to be feeling much too carefree. It was probably from not having any sleep and drinking too much of that Highland whisky called Mountain Magic. He pulled Holly to her feet and dragged her out to the middle of the floor to dance.

"Percival, nay. I can't dance."

"Of course you can. I insist."

"Nay! You don't understand. I don't know how to do it," she whispered.

He squinted at her and made a face. "You don't know how? Really?"

"Well, I know how commoners dance, but I'm sure it isn't the same as the way nobles do it."

"It's easy. Just follow my lead." He grabbed her and pulled her closer.

He was a good dancer, even when drunk, and this impressed Holly. However, she was a little tipsy from too much wine. Between that and her lack of experience, she kept stepping on his feet and stumbling, not able to get the timing right.

"Ooooh!" she cried out, losing her balance when Percival spun her around too fast. She was going down and could do nothing to stop it. Percival's strong arms were there instantly to catch her and to keep her from hitting the floor and embarrassing herself even more. He held her protectively in a lunge, staring down at her as she stared up at him. With their eyes interlocked, nothing in the world mattered. Everyone else in the room and all the voices seemed to fade away. Then, as if in one of her dreams, he slowly leaned closer and lowered his mouth to hers. Her eyes closed as their lips met, melding together as if that was where they truly belonged. He kissed her long and passionately, and she honestly never wanted it to end."

With her eyes still closed, she held on to Percival, feeling so safe and so loved that she never wanted to wake up if this were really just a dream. Then the music stopped and she heard the clapping, bringing her back to her senses. Her eyes popped open and still in the lunge, she looked up to see everyone staring down at her. It wasn't a dream, but more like a nightmare. Had she just really kissed Percival, a noble, in front of a hall filled with people? She felt like such a fake wearing the dress of a noble and dancing! She was a liar and an imposter, reveling in the comfort of being in the handsome lord's arms. Holly didn't deserve this. She shouldn't be here and doing the things she was doing. What was the matter with her? She needed to get out of here fast.

"Percival? Percival, let me up," she pleaded. When she looked up at his face his eyes were closed and even though he still held her securely, she swore he was asleep. "Wake up!"

His eyes popped open. "I'm awake! I'm awake, honest I am." He pulled her back to an upright position.

"Congratulations, ye finally used the kissin' bough!" called out Morag from across the room.

"I don't want to hear you griping anymore about Christmas or anything that goes along with it," shouted his brother.

"Holly, I need to use the garderobe." Noel's little face looked up at her as he tugged on her long sleeve.

"I will take him," offered Percival, his eyes closing and his body swaying while he spoke.

"Nay, I will do it," said Holly, putting her hand on him to steady him. "You just sit down and relax before you fall over, being so tired." Holly helped Percival over to the table and got him seated on the bench. She started thinking mayhap it wasn't a good idea to let him bring her here. He should have stayed back at the cabin to sleep, and she and Noel should have stayed where they belonged. As much as she enjoyed the food, the gown, and even the dancing, it all felt wrong. She should have told him she was a serf. If so, he never would be helping her to pretend she was someone she was not. Her stomach twisted into a knot and her head spun with confusion. What was happening to her? And why had she allowed it to happen? Nothing good could come from this, she was sure.

"Hurry back," Percival said with a silly grin, and his eyes closed once more. She took Noel's hand to lead him away and when she looked back, Percival's head was down on the trestle table and he was fast asleep.

"Are you having fun with your new friends?" Holly asked her brother.

"I am," he told her. "I never want to leave."

Mayhap Noel never wanted to leave, but all she wanted to do was to get out of here. Still, how could she do so when Percival was sleeping? She couldn't just leave him here. Could she?

They were on their way back from the garderobe, descending the stairs from the upper floor, when Holly heard a voice that stopped her in her tracks and almost stilled her heart as well.

"I'm looking for a woman named Holly Wakefielde and her young brother, Noel. Have you seen them?" It was Lord Neville, standing at the door to the great hall with several of his men from Kestwick. He was talking to one of Lord Bedivere's castle guards.

"I'm not sure, my lord. There are a lot of people here for the Christmastide celebration," the guard told him. "Are you here visiting as well?"

"Nay, I am not visiting and I am not interested in any silly Christmas celebration. I am Lord Neville Winfield from Castle Kestwick. Two of my serfs have escaped and I am trying to find them."

"Well, I suppose they could be here." The guard looked

back at the great hall. "However, since I don't know them, I really couldn't tell you. But you are welcome to take a look for yourself."

"Don't think I won't," he spat. "And when I find them, I will collect them and bring them back, giving them the punishment they deserve." He turned back to his own guards. "Men, spread out and search every corner. We've looked everywhere else and couldn't find them, so I am sure they must be here."

"Oh, no!" whispered Holly, pulling her brother back into a shadow. She could see into the great hall from their position. Percival's head was still down and he was not moving. She couldn't get back to him if she tried, without Lord Neville or one of his guards seeing and catching them.

"I'll bring you to Lord Bedivere, the lord of the castle," said the guard. "He might know more about your runaway serfs. Follow me, please."

"Noel, we have to leave right now, and you need to be very quiet," Holly told her brother.

"Nay, I don't want to go without Percival."

"Percival is sleeping and he can take care of himself."

"But Holly, I can't leave Henry and his friends," he said, speaking about his toys.

"Our lives depend on this, Noel. Now forget about the toys and let's get out of here." She held on to his hand and started for the door, keeping an eye open for any of Lord Neville's guards.

Noel broke away from her, meaning to go back into the great hall for his toys.

"No, you don't!" Holly darted forward and grabbed his arm, pulling him back the other way. "We'll get them later.

We can't let Lord Neville see us. Now, come. We must leave."

"What about Percival? Isn't he coming with us? He can protect us from Lord Neville."

"Not now, he can't," she said, wishing he was awake because then he might be able to do something in their favor. But as soon as Lord Neville told Lord Bedivere who she really was, she realized there would be no hope for them at all. Once the nobles of Rothbury Castle found out they'd been harboring a serf, they would be eager to turn them in. It was expected of them and there would be no reason to act differently.

Holly felt so alone. What had started out as a wonderful dream was quickly turning into a nightmare. She needed to protect her brother and they needed to leave the castle now. The only thing was, she wasn't sure where to go or what to do. "Oh, Percival," she whispered, wanting to feel protected in his arms right now. Then again, once he knew the truth about her, he would probably turn her in as well.

She pulled her crying brother along with her, making her way out into the cold without a cloak and over to the stables. Entering the stables, she saw a horse saddled and ready to ride. She didn't hesitate. This was her answer and her only way out of here. She didn't care whose steed it was, she was going to use it for their escape.

"Climb up, Noel," she said, first helping her brother into the saddle and then pulling herself up after him. It wasn't easy to do while wearing the long gown. Plus, she sat astride which wasn't ideal for the way she was dressed either.

"We should wait for Percival," said Noel. "He'll bring Henry and his friends for me, I know he will."

"Percival is not coming, so forget about him." She grabbed the reins and turned the horse.

"I'm cold, Holly." The little boy's body shivered.

"Just snuggle up close to me and I'll keep you warm," she told him, using Willow's warm gown that she was wearing to help protect her brother from the cold.

"Hey, what are you doing?" shouted the stable boy, running toward her. "That is Lord Neville's horse."

Of all the horses to take, it had to be his! Well, she didn't have a choice now. She had to get out of there quickly. Kicking her heels into the horse's sides, she rode it hard and fast into the dark night. Thoughts filled her head of what Lord Neville would do to them once he caught them. Running away was by far punishable enough to make her cringe. But stealing the lord's horse on top of that was certainly going to cost her a finger or two.

The snow came down and the wind continue to blow. Holly was chilled to the bone and her little brother shivered uncontrollably in her arms. Her teeth chattered. With nowhere else to go, and being lost in the dark of night, Holly found herself returning to the only place she knew she could find. She rode straight for Imanie's cottage in the secret garden. She only prayed that no one would tell Lord Neville about this place. Even if it only bought her a little time until the sun rose, she hoped she would be safe here for the night.

Closing the garden gate behind her, she stabled the horse and then carried her brother into the house.

"I-I'm so c-cold, H-Holly." Neville's little body felt like ice. Her heart went out to him.

"Get in bed, right under the covers. I'll crawl in with you and we'll keep each other warm."

"Light the fire," he told her, but she didn't want to do that. If Lord Neville and his guards were out searching for her, they would see or smell the smoke and it would lead them right to them.

"Nay, we can't, I'm sorry," said Holly, crawling into bed and pulling the covers up and over their heads.

"It's so dark. I'm scared. Light the candle, Holly. Please."

"I don't want Lord Neville to see the light, Noel. We'll have to stay in the dark until morning."

Noel started to cry. "I wish Henry was here. I need Henry. I want Percival too."

"I'm sure Percival will watch over Henry for you, now go to sleep."

Holly held her brother close, feeling the drumming of both of their rapidly beating hearts. She was cold and frightened, just as he was. They were all alone now, and it was such a sad and empty feeling. She wanted Percival here. She needed him. What started out as a wonderful day ended horribly. Now, she could only wait for the light of day and then hopefully ride to another town with Noel and hide there, hoping Lord Neville would never find her.

"Oh, Percival," she whispered, a tear trailing down her cheek. Now, she regretted not telling him she was a runaway serf in the first place. He was a good man and deserved the truth. He would hate her now and think she purposely deceived him to get what she wanted, when that was the furthest thing from the truth. She couldn't blame him if he no longer wanted anything to do with her. She didn't deserve the man's care and attention. She realized she could never see him again after this. It would only put him and his family in danger if she did. They'd be accused of harboring a runaway serf, and that would only bring more trouble.

Her heart ached. Wearing the gown of a lady, eating the food of the nobles, and being part of the wonderful family Christmas celebration, for a short time Holly had fooled herself. She thought things could be different and that she could be happy. Her mother wanted a better life for Holly and Noel, and Holly had tried to get it. She had even dreamed that she and Noel could spend the rest of their lives in this cabin along with Percival.

But dreams such as this were not for the poor, the peasants, or the lonely. She fingered the heart brooch pinned to her chest, wanting to be a strong woman like her mother, but not feeling strong at all right now. If only she had really been a member of the Followers of the Secret Heart instead of just a serf, mayhap her life could be different. Mayhap somehow she could have been happy for good instead of just for such a short, short while.

CHAPTER TEN

"**B**rother, wake up!" Percival was in the middle of a dream involving making love with Holly, when his brother's voice disturbed him.

"Go away," he mumbled with a swipe of his arm, wanting to go back to his dream.

"Percival, ye need to wake up. Holly is in trouble," said Morag.

"What?" Percival's eyes snapped open. Everyone was sideways. That's when he realized he'd been sleeping with his head down on the trestle table in the great hall of Rothbury Castle. "Holly. Where's Holly?"

He bolted upright, his hand hitting something and sending it skittering across the table. He looked down to see Noel's wooden toys. "What's going on?" he asked, not seeing Noel either. "Are Holly and Noel back from the garderobe yet?" He vaguely remembered something like that, but honestly wasn't quite sure. His eyes felt sunken in his face and his head hurt like the devil.

"Percival, Lord Neville Winfield from Kestwick is here,

asking a lot of questions about Holly and Noel," said Willow. God's eyes, who wasn't standing over him right now?

"Lord Neville?" Why did that name sound so familiar?

"It seems Holly and Noel are runaway serfs. Lord Neville is here to collect what is his," explained Bedivere.

"What?" Percival was wide awake now. And now he knew why that name sounded so familiar. Noel had said that Rothbury Castle was so much bigger than Lord Neville's castle. Plus, Holly had told him that they lived in Kestwick. God's eyes, he hoped he was still dreaming because there is no way he wanted this to be true.

"Percival, is it true?" asked his mother, making him groan inwardly that she was here too. "Were you harboring runaway serfs?"

"That's highly punishable," said Morag's cousin, Maira. "I hear those who harbor an escaped serf receives the same punishment as the serf."

"That's true," agreed Bedivere. "And it has been known to happen. It's not a pretty ending for either the serf or the one who helped them."

"Wait a minute." Percival tried to stand up too quickly and almost fell over and sat back down. "I didn't know they were runaway serfs. Holly didn't tell me that."

"Of course, she didn't," said Bedivere, sounding disgusted. "Just like you didn't tell her about being in prison. I told you the girl was hiding something and you didn't want to listen to me."

"I told him the same thing," said Maira, making Percival want to send them all away.

"So, I lent a serf one of my best gowns?" gasped Willow, sounding horrified at the thought.

"Where is she? Where's Holly?" Percival slowly stood up and looked around the room. There were servants sleeping on the floor. It was barely daybreak. He could see the sun starting to rise. "Oh, hell. Is it already morning?"

"Yes, it is," said his mother.

"And Holly and Noel are missin'," added Morag's sister, Fia.

"What about Lord Neville? Where is he and what did you tell him?" Percival blurted out. "I will personally kill anyone who leads this devil to Holly and Noel."

"Calm down, Brother." Bedivere placed his hand on Percival's arm. "I played dumb, but I think Kestwick knows I was lying."

"If anything happens to Holly or Noel, there will be hell to pay." Percival got up and started pacing back and forth.

"Ye've go to find them before Lord Neville does," said Morag.

"Where do you think they went?" asked his mother.

The squire, Branton, entered the great hall, walking up to join them. "I just came from the stable," he said. "Lord Bedivere, did you know there is a man named Lord Neville Winfield from Castle Kestwick here looking for a couple of his runaway serfs? It seems they even stole his horse. He's furious about it."

"Yes, Branton, we know," said Maira through clenched teeth. "He is looking for Holly and Noel."

"Who?" asked Branton.

"Holly is Percival's girl, and Noel is her little brother," Morag explained. "Ye ken. The lassie and the little boy we saw in Imanie's secret garden?"

"Oh, them? Uh oh," said Branton, seeming suddenly uncomfortable.

"What the hell does that mean?" Percival stopped pacing.

"Branton, did you do something?" asked Maira.

"Please tell me you didn't." Percival held his breath waiting for Branton to answer.

"I didn't realize it was them, I swear. But when the man asked me if there was anywhere around here for runaway serfs to hide, I told him the only place possible that I could think of, which was the cottage at the secret garden. I told him where to find it, and he and his men left, heading in that direction."

"Nay, you fool!" screamed Percival, lunging at the squire, but Bedivere stepped in to block him from killing the boy.

"Stop it, Percival. He didn't know," said Bedivere in a deep voice.

"He did know! He saw them there," snarled Percival. "And that is probably right where Holly took Noel. She wouldn't know where else to go in the cold and the dark. God's eyes, how can this be happening?"

"I'm truly sorry. I was never introduced to them and I didn't know they meant something to you," apologized Branton.

"He's going to find them and kill them." Percival ran a hand through his hair, trying harder than ever to think straight, but it wasn't easy after having had little sleep and too much Mountain Magic. "Why didn't someone wake me last night when this first happened?"

"We tried," said Morag. "But we couldn't."

"You were dead to the world," said Bedivere with a nod.

"I've got to find her before that bastard does." Percival scooped up Noel's toys from the table and stuck them into his pouch. "I fear I might already be too late."

"Percival, what can you really do?" asked his mother. "They are runaway serfs and belong to Lord Neville."

"He's right," said Willow. "You can't get involved."

"If you do, it might bring upon a battle between Kestwick and us," added Bedivere. "God's eyes, why did you have to fall for someone who is only a serf?"

"Bedivere! How can ye say that?" scolded Morag. "I fell in love with ye and I knew ye were an assassin. This isna as bad as that at all. Holly and Noel are scared and all alone. Ye've got to help Percival find them."

"I agree," said Fia. "Holly and Noel might be serfs, but they are still good people. We've all got to help them."

"Thank you," said Percival, grateful for his family's offer to help. "However, I can't ask any of you to do that. It is too risky for you. I will take the fall for this. Only I will be punished for harboring runaway serfs, and that is the way it is going to be."

"Why does anyone need to punished for it?" asked Maira.

"It's the rules. You know that," answered Willow.

"She's right, but if anyone can break the rules and walk away as victors, it is this family," Branton spoke up. "I, for one, want to help Percival find and protect them."

"He's right about our family breaking rules and still living a good life," said Percival with a nod. "I intend to not only find Holly and Noel, but will do so much more than that. Excuse me." He pushed past the others, hearing his brother call out from behind.

"Percival? What are you going to do? Percival!"

He didn't stop and neither did he turn around. Instead, he rushed out to the stable to get his horse and to do whatever the hell it took to make sure Holly and Noel would never have to answer to the wicked Lord of Kestwick again.

"HOLLY, wake up. I hear hoofbeats. I think Percival is back."

Holly heard her brother and sprang out of bed, not even realizing she had fallen asleep. She'd hugged Noel throughout the night, never even starting a fire or lighting a candle for fear they'd be spotted.

"Percival?" She ran over to the window where Noel had already opened the shutters and was looking out. She hoped to see Percival, but instead she saw Lord Neville and two of his guards heading toward the stable. A third guard was already inside the barn and came running out.

"Your horse is inside the stable, my lord," the guard shouted.

"Good. Good," chuckled Lord Neville. "That means they must be in the house. Let's go get them, shall we?"

"God's eyes, nay!" Holly quickly shut and locked the shutter and paced back and forth.

"Is he going to punish us for running away?" asked Noel with sad eyes. "I don't want to go back to Kestwick. I want to stay here with you and Percival. Holly, don't let them take us back."

"Hush, Noel. I am trying to think." She continued to pace, fingering the heart brooch on her bodice. Then, almost as if she could hear the voice of her dead grandmother, she heard... or mayhap thought... that they needed to get out of the cottage and hide somewhere until Lord Neville left.

"Holly, what are we going to do?" asked Noel.

"Fast, put on your shoes," she told him, helping the little boy. They didn't have cloaks or anything to wear to keep them from the cold since they'd left them at Rothbury Castle. She could take a blanket but it was bright colors and would be too easy to spot. "We are going to hide outside until Lord Neville and his men leave. But I need you to remain really quiet, Noel. No matter what happens, you have to promise to stay silent."

Noel started to cry. "I want Mother."

"Please, Noel. You need to cooperate. Now, let's sneak out a back window so they won't see us."

"All right," agreed the little boy. "But why isn't Percival here to help us?"

Holly wondered the same thing, feeling a little disappointed. The only thing she could think of was that Percival found out they were runaway serfs and wanted nothing to do with them ever again.

She took Noel out a back window softly closing the wooden shutter behind her. Her eyes were drawn to the standing wooden grave markers of Imanie and Mazelina. They would be able to get behind them easily and they were large enough to cover their presence. Or at least she hoped so.

She got Noel over to the graves, but realized that their tracks in the snow could be easily followed. Picking up a dead branch of a tree, she went back and used it to brush away their tracks and then hunkered down behind the grave markers with her brother.

"Shhh," she told her brother, holding a finger to her lips.

She could hear Lord Neville and his men. They were going through the house looking for them. Things crashed and broke inside, and then the door slammed open.

"They aren't in the house so they must be out here," announced Lord Neville. "Search the grounds and also the barn. They can't have gone far. I want them found and returned to me. Do you all understand?"

"Yes, my lord," answered his guards. She kept her head down, holding her brother, hearing the guards run past the grave and toward the barn.

Holly's heart beat so loudly that she was sure Lord Neville could hear it. Then, just when she started thinking that mayhap they'd gotten away with this, Lord Neville reached behind the grave marker and pulled Noel to his feet.

"I've got them," shouted Neville. "Over here."

Noel kicked and screamed and tried to get away.

"Leave my brother alone!" Holly rushed out from her hiding place and grabbed Noel and pushed him behind her.

"Such a brave little serf." Neville laughed in her face and grabbed her hair and twisted. She screamed out in pain and fell to her knees in the snow.

"Why are you wearing the gown of a noble?" asked Neville. "Hamilton must have given it to you. I knew they were lying. They'll be punished for this too and will curse the day they decided to help you."

"Nay! Don't hurt Percival and let go of my sister!" Noel rushed at him and when he did, Neville grabbed him with his other hand.

"Guards! Get over here. Where the hell are you?" shouted Neville.

"They're a little tied up right now," came a voice that

Holly knew only too well. Still cringing in pain, she glanced up to see Percival throwing one of the guards into the snow next to two others. They had their legs and arms tied with rope.

"What?" Lord Neville turned in surprise. "How did you do that by yourself?"

"He wasn't alone," came another voice, and Bedivere walked up next to his brother. Holly saw Branton, the squire, holding his sword over the three guards lying in the snow.

"Percival!" Holly cried, tears of joy in her eyes.

"Let them go, Neville," warned Percival.

"Nay. These are my serfs. You have no right to tell me what to do with them. I'll have your head for this."

There was commotion at the garden gate and a large group of people entered. Holly saw Lady Maira atop a horse with her sword drawn. Lady Morag and Lady Willow were on horses right behind her. And with them were their fathers, Lords Reed, Rowen, and Rook, the Legendary Bastards of the Crown.

"God's eyes, not the Bastards," spat Neville, letting go of Holly but not Noel. Holly ran over to stand with Percival who had his sword drawn.

"Now the boy," commanded Percival. "Let him go as well."

"Nay, I won't do that," said Neville. "This one, I have a personal interest in."

"What the hell does that mean?" growled Bedivere, holding an ax and coming closer.

"This one," said Neville, calling out loud enough for the Legendary Bastards to hear as well. "This one is more than just a serf to me. You see, Noel is also my son."

CHAPTER ELEVEN

"He is not your son!" shouted Percival, looking over to see the odd expression on Holly's face. "Holly? What is it?"

"I'm sorry, Percival, but he really is Noel's father. Lord Neville forced himself on my mother. It wasn't a mutual coupling."

"Nay! I don't want you for my father." Noel stomped on Neville's foot and bit his hand. He managed to wiggle loose and rushed over to Holly who gathered him up into her arms.

"It doesn't matter what any of you want. The whelp is from my seed and he'll return with me to Kestwick. The girl, on the other hand, will be put in the dungeon and lose a few fingers for trying to escape."

"Nay!" cried Morag from atop her horse. "Da, do somethin'."

Reed got off his horse, followed by his brother Rowen. Rook went over to help Branton with the guards. The triplets were big men and could fight like no other. If there was going to be a battle, it was good that they were there.

"Kestwick, let them go," commanded Reed.

"I can't do that." Neville looked up and laughed. "Ah, the rest of my guards are here. Good. Come get the girl and the boy and let's get back to Kestwick."

"Nay! Take me back and punish me if you must, but let Noel stay here with Percival," begged Holly. "He is just a child. I made him come with me, it wasn't his choice. Besides, he doesn't want to live with an evil man like you, even if you are his father."

"He's my bastard and all bastards one day reunite with their fathers, isn't that right?" he asked looking directly at Reed and Rowen.

"No' all of them," spat Reed, pulling his sword, ready for a fight.

"Wait!" Percival held out his arm to stop him. "There must be some way we can come to an agreement. Please. Let's talk about this."

"There is nothing to talk about," was Kestwick's answer. "Holly's father was a serf indentured into my service, and so she shall also be for the rest of her life. The boy, on the other hand will be taken to the castle where I will raise him since he is my son and has half-noble blood running through his veins."

"Nay, you won't." One of Neville's older guards came forward atop his horse. "I have remained silent for too long and will not do so anymore."

"Lord Henry, step down," warned Neville.

"Henry? That's the name of my horse." Noel looked up at Holly with sad eyes.

"Lord Neville, I don't care what you do to me, but I will no longer keep silent." Lord Henry, a large, dark-haired man got off his horse. He nodded to Percival, Bedivere, and the others, and walked up to confront Lord Neville. Looking out to the crowd, he spoke loudly. "I want it to be known that I, Sir Henry Winfield of Kestwick, am Lord Neville's half-brother."

"What do we care?" asked Reed. "This has nothin' to do with the girl and her brother."

"Give me a second," said Lord Henry, raising his hand. "You see, I was in love with a woman who was first the lover of my friend, the castle serf, Preston Wakefielde."

"Keep quiet, Henry," warned Neville, but the man kept talking.

"You are speaking of our mother, Eve," said Holly.

"Yes," he confirmed with a nod. "Holly, do you know anything about your father?"

"Nay," she said with a shake of the head. "I asked my mother but she just said he died in a plowing accident, being kicked by a horse. It happened when I was very young. I don't remember much of him at all."

"Well, that's a lie. I'm sure your mother told you that because she didn't want you to ever know that your father was whipped and beaten by my brother because he didn't bring in a large enough crop one year. Preston sadly died from those inflicted wounds."

"Nay!" Holly gasped and covered her mouth with her hand.

"Enough!" shouted Neville, growing red in the face. "He was only a serf. It doesn't matter."

"It matters to me, and it certainly must have mattered to my mother," said Holly, trying to hold back her tears.

"Go on," Bedivere urged Sir Henry. "Tell us the rest."

"I will," said Henry. "I found out that Eve was part of a secret group of women."

"That's right. She was." Holly's hand covered the heart brooch.

Henry continued. "She helped deliver babies, not only to the serfs and nobles, but to all the women who were impregnated by my brother's seed. Especially the ones who were left widows by his hand when his temper flared."

"Stop it," shouted Neville. "Besides, what does any of this matter? Every lord of a castle has the right to do what he wants. He also has the right to his bastards."

Henry glared at his brother. "Mayhap so, but not twenty bastards—the number of babies you sired from bedding your servants and serfs."

"God's eyes, Kestwick, you disgust me," said Percival through gritted teeth.

"If you want to claim one of your rightful bastards, then do so," Henry told Neville. "But I will no longer let you claim *my* son as your own." He looked over at Noel. "Noel, I am sorry I never spoke up before now. I let my brother rule me in fear because he threatened to kill your mother and sister if the truth ever got out."

"Then Neville didn't force himself on Holly's mother?" asked Percival.

"Nay, he did," answered Henry. "However, it was after she was already pregnant by my seed. He found out about it, and that is why he abducted her." He looked over at Holly. "I am so, so sorry. I came by as often as I could and brought things for your mother and you and Noel. But I should have done more. I see that now and I regret it."

"Henry, we're going. Bring the boy," said Neville, planning to leave.

Suddenly, every man standing there had his hand on his sword.

"Nay," said Henry. "That is not going to happen. I will not let you rule me anymore." He looked at Noel. "Son, you don't deserve the way I acted and I am sorry I couldn't tell you the truth. But I loved your mother, and I loved you ever since the day you were born. I just couldn't show it or acknowledge it, because of my brother. No matter, you deserve better. And you certainly don't deserve to go with my brother because he will never treat you as well as I will, if you'll give me that chance to make up for my past mistakes."

"You'll never have that chance because I won't allow it," growled Neville. Standing behind Henry, Neville drew his sword to his brother's back, meaning to strike him down dead.

"Sir Henry! Behind you," shouted Percival, causing Henry to turn and draw his sword at the same time. There was the sickening sound of metal sinking into flesh and then blood spurted everywhere, staining the snow red.

"Don't look, Noel!" instructed Holly, pulling her crying brother to her, hiding his eyes from the gruesome sight.

"God's eyes, nay!" Percival was the first to reach the fallen men, with Bedivere and Reed right behind him.

"What's going on?" yelled Rook from over by the tied-up guards. The rest of Neville's men dismounted and drew their swords. A fight was inevitable.

"Lower your swords," called out Sir Henry, holding his bleeding side, trying to sit up with Percival's help.

"We don't answer to you," snapped one of the guards. "We only take orders from Lord Neville."

"Lord Neville is dead," announced Bedivere with his hand to the man's neck, looking for a pulse. He had been stabbed right through the heart by his brother. "Sir Henry has killed him."

All were silent for a minute.

"Then ye are Lord of Kestwick now?" Reed asked Henry.

"Aye. I suppose I am," Henry answered, struggling to breathe. And as Lord of Kestwick, I command... I command..." Lord Henry's eyes closed and his head fell back onto Percival's lap as he fell unconscious.

"He's losing a lot of blood. We need to get him into the cottage and sew him up quickly." Percival started to lift Henry with Bedivere and Reed helping him.

"Lords Rowen and Rook," Bedivere called out. "Take Lord Neville's body back to the castle along with Lord Neville's men. Send back a healer. Branton, untie the guards."

"Untie them? Are you sure about this?" asked Rook.

"Go!" shouted Bedivere. "And take the women, too."

"Nay!" said Morag, getting off her horse. "I will stay here with Holly. She might need me."

"Yes, me too," added Willow, and Maira nodded. None of them were going anywhere. They were staying to help Holly and that meant the world to her.

"Thank you," said Holly, nodding to the ladies who she now considered her new friends. Then she looked back at the dying man who was Noel's father. "However, I am fine. I am strong," she said, running her fingers over the heart pin and looking over at her grandmother's grave next. She knew what her mother or grandmother would do in this situation and that is exactly what she would do, too.

"Please, watch over Noel and get some water heated over the fire instead."

"Water? What for?" asked Willow.

"I saw a sewing kit in my grandmother's cupboard and I am going to stich up Lord Henry's wound. Maira, can you tear up the sheets on the bed so we can use them as bandages?"

"Right away," said Maira, hurrying toward the house.

"Ye are goin' to sew him up?" asked Morag. "Why dinna ye wait for the healer to come from the castle to do that?"

"I don't want to wait," said Holly. "If we wait, it might be too late and Lord Henry could die. And even if I never had the chance to really know my father, I will do anything in my power to save the life of Noel's father so he at least has the chance that he deserves to know his."

CHAPTER TWELVE

Holly paced back and forth later that night, after having done everything she could to help save Sir Henry's life. The healer had arrived as well, and said she did a good job sewing the man up. The healer told her if she hadn't done so, Lord Henry would have lost too much blood and died before he even got there.

Ladies Willow and Maira had gone back to the castle, but Morag stayed. So did Bedivere. Actually, Percival's mother, Ada, arrived with Morag's father, Reed, and a lot of food that was leftover from the Christmas dinner which they all ate earlier in silence. No one seemed to want to speak about what had transpired today.

The healer left an hour ago, saying there was nothing more he could do. Whether Sir Henry survived was no longer up to them, but God.

Sir Henry occupied the bed. Noel fell asleep in Percival's arms, holding on to all his little friends made of wood. Holly's heart went out to him. She couldn't imagine what the little boy was even feeling.

"Percival, bring the boy over here," said his mother softly. "I have brought blankets from the castle and made him a bed in the corner."

"Aye," agreed Percival, putting Noel down, kissing him atop the head and covering him up.

"Would anyone like some hot cider?" asked Ada. "Morag has some heating over the fire."

"I'll take some, but I have a little somethin' to add to it." Reed pulled out a flask and Holly knew there was whisky in it.

"I'll take some of that but without the cider." Bedivere pushed a wooden cup across the table closer to Reed.

"How about ye, Percival?" Reed held up the flask.

"God's teeth, nay," he said, dragging a hand through his hair. "I think I've learned my lesson where Mountain Magic is concerned."

"Why don't you get some sleep?" Holly asked Percival. "You must be very tired."

"I am, but I can't sleep. Not now. Not yet. Holly, will you walk outside with me? I'd like to speak to you in private."

"Of course," said Holly, taking a cloak from Percival's mother. The woman had thought of everything and it was good to have her there.

Percival helped Holly don her cloak and then guided her with his hand to the small of her back, opening the door and leading her out to the porch. Nothing was said until he closed the door and turned back toward her.

PERCIVAL HAD SO much to say to Holly, but he didn't know where to start. With the full moon shining down on her golden tresses, she looked like a Christmas angel to him, if there was such a thing. He was no longer sure. He had decided to make new memories, but this Christmas wasn't getting much better than the one that had haunted him since the death of his father.

"Holly," he said, at the same time she said, "Percival."

"I need to talk to you," he continued.

"Fine, but me first," she told him. "I was wrong in not telling you from the start that I was a runaway serf. I'm sorry. I never should have come here, but when my mother died, I didn't know what to do. She told me to come here. I was just trying to care for my little brother." Her hand covered the heart brooch once more. "I ran away because it was what Mother wanted."

"Nay. It was the right thing to do," agreed Percival.

"Really? Do you really think so?"

"Yes. I wouldn't want you and Noel living under those conditions. It sounds like Lord Kestwick was a horrible man."

"Oh, he was."

"I also wouldn't want Noel living with Lord Neville."

"Well, that won't happen since the man is dead now."

"Aye. And I believe everything turned out exactly as it should."

"I'm still a serf, Percival," she seemed inclined to remind him, even though there was no way he could forget. You realize, that means we can't be together."

"Let's not talk about that right now," he said, taking her hands in his. "It's my turn to talk now."

"There is nothing you need to say. This is all my fault."

"Holly, I'm so sorry that today is such a horrible day for you, being your birthday and also Christmas. I really wanted to make it a special time for you, but everything turned to hell."

"It's all right, Percival. You were so kind and did so many things for me and Noel and I can never thank you enough. You are a good man."

"Mayhap not as good as you think. You see, I haven't been totally honest with you, either."

"What do you mean?"

"I mean... I was imprisoned for a while. My entire family was, actually."

"Imprisoned? For what? Did you murder someone?"

"Nay. Of course not."

"Were you trying to kill the king like your father was?"

"No! And to clarify things, he was falsely accused. I can tell you more about it at a later date. I just wanted you to know I was in prison. Oh, and my brother, Bedivere was an assassin too."

"Is this all real?" she asked with a small grin. "Or are you saying this just trying to make me feel better? Because it is one hell of a story."

"Nay, it's true. I can tell you all about it."

"Nay, no need," she said, holding up a hand. "Someday, mayhap, but right now, I don't even care about any of that."

"You don't?"

"Nay, Percival. I like you for who you are now. I also like your entire family very much. I know in my heart you are all good, fair people. You see, I don't care who or what you used to be. All that matters is what is happening right now, in the precious present."

"I like you for the wonderful woman you are as well, Holly."

"Even though I'm naught but a serf?" Her eyes filled with tears.

"Especially since you are a serf," he told her, kissing her hands.

"Percival, you make no sense at all." With a half-smile she wiped the tears from her eyes.

"Holly, you showed me that I was living in a world of doom because I couldn't move on from the past. I hated Christmas because it reminded me of my father being killed on that day."

"And now you have a new reason to hate it even more, don't you? And it is all because of me."

"No, just the opposite, actually."

"Huh?" She blinked several times in succession, trying to understand him.

"My sweet Holly, because of you I found the joy and spirit of Christmas again. I discovered by being with you and Noel what's important and what is not. What really matters. Because of you, I realize I don't need to be so bitter and hateful. You find joy in the smallest things, and I love that about you. I also love your strong sense of the importance of family and your love of family traditions. I want to do that too, from now on."

"Well, you have a large family and can certainly do that even without me."

"Not without you, I can't."

"I don't understand."

"I-I think I love you, Holly. I never thought I'd say this to any woman, but I really think I have fallen in love with you."

"Oh, Percival." She started to cry. "I think I love you, too."

He chuckled. "Then why are you crying? That's a good thing, isn't it?"

"If I were a noble, or you were a serf, then mayhap it would be. But we can never be together and you know that is the truth. Now, let's go inside and try to get some sleep. God knows you need it more than anyone."

Percival didn't like the way they left off, but needed to think about this more, and with a clear head. Holly was right. Mayhap after some sleep he could come up with a solution that would make both of them happy for the rest of their lives.

CHAPTER THIRTEEN

Holly awoke to the sound of laughter, which confused her more than anything. At first, she thought she was only dreaming. Then she opened her eyes, and from her spot on the floor next to her brother, she saw Percival and Bedivere sitting at Lord Henry's bedside. The wounded knight was propped up and his eyes were wide open. He was no longer unconscious!

"Percival?" She rubbed one eye.

"Holly, come here," said Percival, sitting on the edge of the bed and holding out his arms.

"I'll have food ready soon to break the fast," said Ada from the hearth. She and Morag were cooking over the open flames.

"Where is Willow?" asked Holly.

"She left with my da last night and went back to the castle," Morag told her, peeking into a pot over the fire and using a big wooden spoon to stir the contents. "Ye didna really think Willow would sleep on the floor, did ye?"

That made Percival and Bedivere laugh.

"I don't know. I just met her." Holly got to her feet.

"Believe me, she wouldna," said Morag making a face, heading back to the table to set up the wooden bowls.

"Holly, come here. Please." Percival patted his lap, meaning for her to sit down.

"I-I can get a chair." She wasn't sure she felt comfortable enough around the men to do such a thing.

"No, you won't." Percival pulled her over to him and atop his lap. "I'm a better chair, anyway."

"Good morning, Holly," said Sir Henry. He was smiling and the color had come back to his face. "Thank you for stitching me up yesterday. I heard it is you I have to thank for not letting me bleed to death waiting for the healer to arrive."

"Anyone would have done the same as I did. I should check your wound." She reached for his bandage, but Percival pulled her back.

"Mother already did that. The bleeding has stopped," Percival told her.

"Plus, the healer will be here shortly," Ada called out from the fire.

"How are you feeling?" asked Holly.

"Much better now that I know I'm going to live." That made the men laugh and Henry held his side, telling her that it hurt to laugh.

Holly used to see Lord Henry at their home from time to time while growing up, and now she knew why. Her mother had always called him her friend, but never said anything more. Lord Henry had always been kind to her, as well as to her brother. Noel might not remember him, having been so young, but she still thought Henry must have made a good impression on him since he named his toy horse after him.

"Lord Henry, will you someday tell me more about my father?" asked Holly. "I would really like to hear about him."

"I will, I promise," said Henry. "However, you'll have to come visit me in Kestwick in order for me to tell you all the stories I have of your father. Most nobles aren't friends with serfs; however, I guess you can say I am different from the rest. Preston was a good man."

"Did you say when I come to visit you in Kestwick?" Her eyes darted back and forth from Henry to Percival. "I'll already be living there. Won't I?"

"Nay, I'm afraid not," said Henry. "I mean, only if you want to, that is."

"I'm afraid I don't understand. I am a serf. I don't have a choice."

"Percival and I have been talking," said Henry. "I have agreed to let him buy your freedom from me. So you see, you are no longer a serf and bound to my land. You, my dear, are a free woman."

"What?" Her eyes opened wide in surprise and her gaze shot over to Percival. "You did that?"

"That's right, Holly. He wrapped his arms around her tighter, almost as if he thought she was going to get away. "You see, I thought of a way for us to be together after all."

"I still don't quite understand. Why would you do that?"

"God's eyes, Brother, just come out and tell her," said Bedivere.

"All right. I will." Percival cleared his throat and then took her hands and stared directly into her eyes. "Holly, I want to marry you. I would like us to be husband and wife and live at Rothbury Castle from now on."

"Serfs need the permission of their lord to get married,"

she said without thinking, not yet used to, or perhaps not really believing she was free.

"Holly, didn't you hear Lord Henry?" asked Percival. "You don't need his permission because you are no longer a serf of Kestwick."

"For the record, I give my permission anyway, even though you don't need it," said Henry.

"Oh," she said, feeling happy yet sad at the same time.

"I was expecting a little more of a positive response than that." Percival pulled away, but she grabbed his shoulders and looked directly into his eyes.

"Of course, I want to be your wife, Percival. I told you, I love you. So that should go without saying."

"Then, why don't you seem as happy as I feel about all this?"

"Well..." She looked over at Lord Henry. "What about my brother, Lord Henry? Where will he be living?"

"With me, of course," said Henry. "At my castle in Kestwick. He'll be raised as my son."

"Holly, I don't want to live with that man." With his toys clasped in his little fists, Noel ran over to Holly for protection. She jumped up and picked him up in her arms, latching him to her hip.

"Noel, Lord Henry is your father," she told him. "It is only right that you should live with him and get to know him."

"I have my good friend, Henry the horse. I don't want another friend named Henry. I don't want to live with him. I want to stay with you." The little boy shyly buried his face against her shoulder.

"Oh, my. I think I made a mess of things," said Henry. "I

can't blame the boy for not wanting to live with me. He doesn't even know me. I guess I just figured... I understand," said Henry, the happiness draining from his face. "Perhaps in time, things will change and you will change your mind, Noel. I truly hope so because I would like to start being a good father to you. That is, the father I always wanted to be."

Holly looked at Percival and shrugged. She didn't know what to do and wanted this to be a happy ending for everyone.

"Noel," said Percival, getting up off the bed. "Where do you want to live?"

"I want to live here. In grandmother's house," said the little boy.

"Here?" Percival smiled. "But this is such a little cottage. You have the chance to live in a big castle and have your own bedchamber."

"I share a bed with Holly," said Noel, not sounding excited at all about this opportunity.

"There will be lots of children for you to play with," Percival told him. "Children your own age. You will make lots and lots of new friends."

"Will you be there with me?" asked Noel.

"Me?" asked Percival. "Well... no. My home is here in Rothbury."

"It doesn't have to be," said Henry. "You and Holly are welcome to live at Kestwick. I'll give you your own chamber right in the castle. Then you will be there with Noel so he won't feel lonely."

"Noel?" Holly looked at her little brother. "How does that sound?"

He looked at his toy horse and pretended the animal was

whispering to him. "Henry says we can go there sometimes, but only if we can stop back home and pick up the rest of his friends."

"Of course, we can," said Percival, ruffling the boy's hair.

"What do you mean by *sometimes*?" asked Holly.

"I like the cottage," said the boy. "It feels like... like home."

"So do I," agreed Holly, not sure she'd ever be able to get used to life at the castle. It was so different than the life she knew. She wasn't used to such grandeur or such fancy meals. While living somewhere besides a small hovel would be nice, she really didn't need all the other frivolities that nobles were used to. "Percival, couldn't we just live here?" she asked him.

"Here? In this broken-down hovel, when we have two castles to choose from?" Percival looked and sounded repulsed, as well as a little forlorn.

Bedivere burst out laughing.

"I don't think it's funny," said Percival. "There isn't enough room here for me to even sleep in the same bed as my wife."

"Percival, really," said Holly, feeling a flush wash over her cheeks.

"There would be enough room if you expanded the place," said Henry from the bed. "There is plenty of room since you're in the woods."

"You could even extend the garden," suggested Ada.

"I'll pay for the workers to build it and make it larger," said Henry. "But only if Noel promises to come stay with me sometimes so we can get to know each other."

"What do you say, Noel?" asked Holly.

"What does *he* say? How about asking *me*?" complained Percival.

"Shush, Percival," his mother told him. "I want to hear my grandson's answer."

"Grandson?" asked Noel. "Will you be my new grandmother?"

"I know I'm not really your grandmother, Noel, but I'd love to pretend you were my grandson," Ada told him with the kindest of smiles.

"All right," said Noel. Then he held up a finger. "Wait." He pretended to listen to his horse again. "Henry says only if we can make the barn bigger and get a couple more horses."

"God's eyes," griped Percival. "Next thing I know you're going to want pigs and chickens and even a dog."

"A dog?" asked Noel with a big smile. "Yes, I want a dog."

"You know, Noel, I have almost a dozen dogs in the kennels at the castle," Henry told him. "Do you think you'd like to see them sometime?"

"I would, I would."

Henry smiled again. "I would like that also. It is a start, anyway."

Once more, Noel listened to his wooden horse, "Henry says you both have the same name."

"Yes. Yes, we do," said Sir Henry. "I like that you named your horse the same as my name. I gave you that horse, but couldn't tell you. So your mother gave it to you for me."

"Oh. Well, Henry doesn't like that you both have the same name," said Noel, shaking his head.

"He doesn't? Why not?" asked Holly.

"Because there can only be one Henry," Noel told him.

"Well, mayhap you should rename your horse," suggested Bedivere.

Noel looked like he was going to cry. Percival threw his brother a daggered look.

"What?" asked Bedivere. "I was only trying to help."

"You can always call me Father instead of Sir Henry." This time it was Henry's suggestion.

Holly held her breath, sure her brother would not agree with that. But after bringing his toy horse to his ear again, the little boy smiled.

"Henry said he likes that idea and so do I... Father."

Holly's heart swelled with glee. It would take some time, but she was sure things would work themselves out in the end.

"How about some pottage?" asked Morag. "It's poured out and ready to eat and is gettin' cold."

"I'll bring your bowl over to you, Sir Henry," said Ada, picking up a bowl and spoon.

"I'll take it to Father. Let me down, Holly. I want to do it." Noel ran over to Ada and together they delivered the food to Henry.

"I think this is all going to work out nicely after all," Holly told Percival, kissing him on the mouth.

"I hope you're talking about the wedding," said Percival. "Because I'm still not so sure about living here at the cottage even if it is expanded."

"Stop squawking, Brother, and sit down and eat," ordered Bedivere. "I'll have everyone from Rothbury help with the building as well. Before we're finished, you'll have a cottage as big as a manor house. Just wait and see what I can do."

EPILOGUE
ONE YEAR LATER, CHRISTMAS

"Percival, hurry. I see Sir Henry and Noel riding into the garden." Holly hurried to the front door, swinging it wide open, excited to see her brother again. The cottage had been expanded, just like everyone promised. It wasn't as large as a manor house, but was elaborate just the same.

Now, where the one-room cottage of Imanie once sat, stood a two-story wooden home with a thatched roof. There were six bedchambers inside, so plenty of room for Noel and even Sir Henry to visit, as well as plenty of room for lots of babies. The barn was attached to the house with a back door leading through a covered walkway because Percival didn't want Holly to become cold going back and forth in the winter. He thought of her every need. Percival even insisted on building a railing around the entire porch which was raised up off the ground. It continued along the side of the cottage, wrapping around all the way to the barn. It was most unusual, but Holly loved it. Percival also said he was thinking and planning ahead. When they had children he wanted to make sure they didn't fall off the porch and hurt themselves.

Of course, Bedivere never stopped teasing him about it, teasing Percival that he was acting more like a wench than a man now. Holly wasn't sure what that meant, but figured it was a private, ongoing thing between the men, and so she didn't even ask.

Percival had become knighted before they were actually wed, because he said he wanted her to marry a knight. And now that he was a knight, he also decided the cottage should be more of a manor house after all. He couldn't seem to stop adding to it. Holly was happy with the original cottage, and didn't need more. But Percival, being a man, was always trying to better himself and the possessions he had. The next thing he was planning to build was a kennel for hunting dogs and a mews, since he once assisted a falconer and was good with birds.

She didn't complain. And even though he did end up telling her all about his past, she never needed to know. She was happy just being with Percival and would never judge him.

It was still hard to believe she was a free woman instead of a serf. It was even harder to believe that the nobles started calling her Lady Holly, giving her a courtesy title even though she wasn't a noble. She heard Percival's family broke the rules of being nobles frequently and got away with things that usually wouldn't be tolerated. Well, this proved it. Of course, since Lady Morag was related to the king, Holly had a hunch the ladies had more to do with this than the men.

Holly looked down to her belly, rubbing it and taking a deep breath. Percival's whole family would be here today and that is the way they wanted it. But before she and Percival told anyone that she was pregnant, she wanted to make sure Noel knew.

Noel was a year older now, and had been spending more and more time with his father. The little boy felt comfortable around Sir Henry, spending weeks at a time living at Castle Kestwick. He had his own dog, a pet goat, a pet goose, and even a frog. He loved animals, and his father loved giving them to him as pets. Noel's latest goal was to become a castle page as soon as he turned seven.

"Everything is ready," said Percival, coming up behind Holly and wrapping his arms around her, giving her a kiss behind her ear. "Are you nervous to tell Noel that we're having a baby?"

"More nervous than I felt telling you," she admitted. "I just don't want Noel to feel like he's being replaced."

"He won't. The boy has a good head on his shoulders. Plus, he gets so much attention from his father that he won't feel like he's being ignored. I hear Noel is trying to find himself a new mother as well."

"That's not true," said Holly. "Noel will never let anyone take the place of Mother."

"That will change," said Percival.

"I don't know about that," said Holly. "After the death of Lord Henry's wife, he fell in love with my mother. He never married again, so what makes you think he will now?"

"Bedivere tells me that every time a lady is kind to Noel, Noel is asking Henry if she is going to be his new mother."

They both laughed at that.

"Henry has his hands full with that boy," said Percival. "You know, I hope we have a little boy just like Noel. I mean, I really miss him now that he doesn't stay with us that often."

"I hope we do, too," admitted Holly. "I really adore my little brother."

Henry and Noel dismounted and walked up to the door. Noel carried a Christmas wreath and handed it to Percival. Holly gave her brother a big hug and also greeted Lord Henry.

"Damn, this looks nice," said Percival, taking the wreath and inspecting it. He never quite did get the hang of creating one.

"Father and I made it for you, Percival," Noel explained.

"Don't you mean you made it for me and Holly both?" asked Percival.

"Nay. Just you," said the little boy. "Holly knows how to make a round wreath and you still need a little practice. So this one is just for you."

They all laughed and went into the house. Holly saw others arriving out the open window and knew she needed to tell Noel about the baby quickly.

"Noel, honey," said Holly. "You know Percival and I are married now and someday I'll be a Mother and Percival will be a Father to a new baby of our own. How do you feel about that?"

"Is she trying to tell us she is going to have a baby?" Noel looked up at his father.

"Yes. Yes, I do believe so," said Henry with a smile.

"This doesn't mean we'll love you any less or that we don't want you. You are still welcome here whenever you want to stay here," Holly made sure to tell him.

"And you can show the baby how to play with wooden

animals, since I plan on making some for all the children we have," added Percival.

"I know," said Noel.

"Are you upset?" asked Holly.

"No. But you'd better take Beauregard the Bear for the new baby." He handed the toy to Percival. "I want to share my toys with the baby when he gets here."

"You would give up one of your toys to the baby?" asked Percival in surprise.

"Yes," answered Noel. "It's all right because I don't care for it much."

"You don't?" asked Holly. "Why not?"

Noel looked up at his father.

"Go ahead and tell him," Henry urged him to speak up. "It is always best to tell the truth."

"You're right, Father." Noel looked like he was reluctant, but told them anyway. "It is not my favorite, because I never thought it looked like a real bear."

"No?" asked Percival.

"Uh uh," said Noel, shaking his head. "I'm sorry, Percival, but I always thought it looked more like a pig instead of a bear."

Holly and Percival looked at each other and started laughing. So, Henrietta the Pig wasn't as misshapen after all. That brought a proud smile to Percival's face.

"Hello, we're here." The door to the cottage opened and Morag walked in with her sister Fia and cousins Willow and Maira. They were all holding their children.

"I didn't know you were all bringing your children," said Percival. "And Mother and Bedivere and the rest of my siblings aren't even here yet. I hope this house is big enough to fit all of us. Mayhap I should have added on another floor."

"No, Percival, the house is fine the way it is," Holly told him. "Any bigger and we'll be calling it a castle instead of just a manor house."

"A castle in the woods," said Percival with a satisfied nod. "I think I like that."

Ada walked in with Bedivere and the rest of Percival's seven siblings pushed into the house as well. Percival's Uncle Theobald and Aunt Joan brought up the rear.

"Branton is stabling all the horses, but said not to wait for him to make the announcement," said Uncle Theobald.

"Announcement?" Holly looked at Percival suspiciously. "What announcement is that, Uncle Theobald?"

"It's my fault," said Morag, looking sheepish. "Och, Holly, I'm sorry but I overheard Percival tellin' Bedivere that ye are pregnant and I just couldna keep it to myself."

"Percival?" Holly's hands went to her hips and her eyes narrowed. "I thought we agreed we were making this announcement together and not until after I told Noel." Holly looked at him from the corners of her eyes and shook her head.

Percival shrugged, holding his palms in the air. "I'm sorry, sweetheart. It might have slipped out when I was talking to my brother, but I was so excited about being a father that I had to tell someone."

All the women started squealing and congratulating Holly while Noel and Percival's younger brothers ran off together to the upstairs rooms to play.

Percival pulled Holly to the side, kissing her under the kissing bough that he insisted they hang up, since he decided he liked them now. Personally, Holly thought it was just Percival's way of getting more kisses than usual. More kisses, that is, that usually ended up with them making love.

"You're not angry with me that I told Bedivere that we're having a baby, are you, sweetheart?" asked Percival, looking so sexy that she couldn't stay mad at the man. "I was so excited that I wanted to shout it to the world, but he's the only one I told. Honest."

"That's right," said Bedivere walking past with his arm around Morag, carrying little Mazelina in the crook of his other arm. "He made me promise to stay silent as well, and I swear I did. But I should have known my busybody little wife was in a shadow listening somewhere."

"Bedivere, I dinna gossip anymore, and ye ken it," said Morag.

"Then what do you call this?" asked Bedivere.

"It is no' gossip if it is true, and I kent it was. Let's just call it spreadin' good news amongst the family."

"It's fine, Morag," Holly assured her. "I'm just happy that my new family is as excited about my pregnancy as I am, and wants to share the news with each other."

"It's still hard to believe that this is the same brother who used to hate Christmas and babies and all things good." Bedivere slapped Percival on the back and headed away.

"That's not true," Percival shouted after him. He looked back to Holly and kissed her again.

Branton walked in, shaking the snow off his boots. "Sir Percival, when did you get a pig?" asked Branton.

"Pig?" Holly frowned. "What pig? We don't have a pig."

"Sure, you do. I'm talking about that big one with the red

bow around its neck in the barn," said Branton. "The sow is so fat that she looks pregnant to me."

"Percival?" Holly looked over at her husband. "I thought we were going to discuss things before we added any more to our home."

"Weeeeeell, I have to know what a pig looks like if I'm going to whittle a toy pig for the new baby. You know how badly the last one turned out. I don't want it looking like a bear again."

She giggled. "I can't stay mad at you."

"I was going to give it to you for a present, but mayhap I'd better give it to Noel instead."

"Good idea," said Holly. "And he can keep all the piglets over at Castle Kestwick once they are born as well."

"That's probably a good idea," Percival agreed.

"You bought the pig and didn't realize it was pregnant, didn't you? Just admit it," said Holly playfully hitting him on the arm.

"You know me too well, Holly. That is what I love about you." He kissed her so passionately she thought he was going to make love to her right there.

"No more secrets, all right?" she made him promise.

"No more pigs, I promise. However, I can't promise anything else."

"Why not?" she asked.

"Because, I didn't tell you about this either." He pulled out a small box from his pouch and she opened it. It was her mother's heart brooch, but there was a diamond embedded in the center.

"Percival, this is beautiful. But why? The brooch was fine the way it was."

"No, it wasn't. You were very strong and brave with everything you went through this past year. I thought you should have your own brooch because you deserve to be in a secret group of strong women."

"Percival, this must have been very expensive. You didn't have to do this, but thank you. I love it."

He helped her pin it onto her gown. "I wanted a diamond on it, since you are the diamond in my life and I don't want you to ever forget it."

"You are the best thing that has ever happened to me, Percival. I thank God every day that we ended up together."

"I am thankful too, Holly. We are married and starting a family together and I couldn't be happier. You taught me what was important in life and how to move on from the past. Thank you. Now tell me, do you really like what I did with the brooch?"

"I do. I love it," she said, holding her hand over the brooch, feeling the presence of both her mother and grand-mother in the house and in her life. She knew they would always be with her in spirit, even though they were not there in body. "My good memories will live on forever, Percival."

"So will mine," he told her. "I now know how to replace the bad ones with the good."

"I love the brooch. I love you, my handsome husband. And although I told you no more secrets, mayhap we should make an exception just at Christmastime."

"I agree," said Percival, putting his hand over her belly. "I will gladly be awaiting many more future *Christmas Secrets*."

A NOTE FROM THE AUTHOR

I hope you enjoyed Percival and Holly's story and will take a minute to leave a review for me. As you've probably noticed from my stories, I like to pair up two people who have no right being together. I also like to embed the spirit of the holidays into my writings whenever I can.

If you like stories that take place or focus on the holiday of Christmas, then be sure to also read **Mistletoe and Chain Mail**, Book 1 of my **Holiday Knights Series,** and **Winter Sage,** Book 5 of my **Below the Salt Series.**

Also, anyone who knows me realizes how much I love my secret garden. I live in the suburbs of Chicago, but have a secret garden in my yard with a writing hammock, where in the nice weather I create my stories from the heart. I was sad when the **Secrets of the Heart Series** ended, so I wanted to write just one more story, tying things together with the recurring characters after **Forgotten Secrets,** Book 4, ended. Percival, brother of Bedivere, showed up in that story, and I decided he needed a romance of his own.

If you'd like to find out more about Sir Bedivere the assassin, he first shows up as more of a villain, in a way, in **Seductive Secrets,** Book 2. I liked the man so much I decided to give him his own story but make him the hero. So, by Forgotten Secrets, Book 4, you see him as the hero, and find out his backstory as to what made him an assassin in the first place. Some of those questions you might have about this might still not be answered after reading **Christmas Secrets**, but I didn't want to give too much away because I want you to enjoy the experience of reading that book for yourself.

Also be sure to read about Morag and Fia's father Reed in **Reckless Highlander**. Willow's father Rook is the hero of **Ruthless Knight**, and Willow's father is Rowen from **Restless Sea Lord.** These are all books of my **Legendary Bastards of the Crown Series** which is one of my favorite series ever. Of course, you'll want to start with the prequel, **Destiny's Kiss,** to find out about the bastard triplets and why they want vengeance against their father, King Edward III.

I have listed a few series for you connected to this story that I think you will enjoy.

Seasons of Fortitude: (The sisters of the Legendary Bastards of the Crown)
   Highland Spring
   Summer's Reign
   Autumn's Touch
   Winter's Flame
   Silent Knight

Legendary Bastards of the Crown: (Fathers of the girls from Secrets of the Heart)
Destiny's Kiss
Restless Sea Lord
Ruthless Knight
Reckless Highlander
Pirate in the Mist

Secrets of the Heart: (Daughters of the Legendary Bastards)
Highland Secrets
Seductive Secrets
Rebellious Secrets
Forgotten Secrets
Christmas Secrets

Please check out my social media as well to find out more about my 100+ books. I write medieval, small town contemporary, paranormal, Western, and fantasy romance.

Elizabeth Rose

Stop by and visit my **Website**. You can follow me on **Amazon**, **Bookbub**, **Goodreads**, **Facebook** and **Twitter**. I also have a **Private Readers' Group** on Facebook that I invite you to join. And don't forget to sign up for my **Newsletter,** so you'll always know right away about my books on sale, for free, new releases, and contests.

ABOUT THE AUTHOR

Elizabeth Rose is an Amazon All-Star, and bestselling, award-winning author of nearly 100 books and counting! Her first book was published back in 2000, but she has been writing stories ever since high school. She is the author of fantasy/paranormal, medieval, small town contemporary, and western romance. You'll find sexy, alpha heroes and strong, independent heroines in her books. Sometimes her heroines can even swing a sword.

Her earlier fantasy romance novels started out with her **Greek Myth Series**, inspired by the TV shows *Legendary Journeys of Hercules* and *Xena: Warrior Princess*. One of the books, **The Oracle of Delphi** was featured on the History Channel during a documentary of the Oracle. Elizabeth joins Oliver Heber Books with her **Portals of Destiny Series** which brings back characters from some of her other fantasy series, making guest appearances.

She loves adding humor to her work, because everyone needs to laugh more in life. Her **Bad Boys of Sweetwater: Tarnished Saints Series,** focuses on 12 brothers, a bunch of kids, and lots of humor. This small-town romance series was inspired by people, places, and things in her own life. The location is the lake and small town of Michigan where she grew up visiting her grandparents.

Living in the suburbs of Chicago with her husband, Elizabeth has two grown sons and one granddog—so far. A lover of nature, she can be found in the summer swinging in her 'writing hammock' in her secret garden, creating her next novel. Her secret garden is what inspired her medieval series, **Secrets of the Heart**, which of course centers around a secret garden too!

Visit Elizabeth's website where you will find book trailers, sneak peeks at upcoming covers, excerpts from her books, as well as original recipes of food that her characters eat in her stories. If you'd like to sign up for her newsletter, join her private readers' group, or follow her on social media, just copy and paste the following links.

Join Elizabeth's Newsletter
Join Elizabeth's Facebook Group

ALSO BY ELIZABETH ROSE

Medieval Series:

Legendary Bastards of the Crown Series

Seasons of Fortitude Series

Secrets of the Heart Series

Legacy of the Blade Series

Daughters of the Dagger Series

MadMan MacKeefe Series

Barons of the Cinque Ports Series

Holiday Knights Series

Highland Chronicles Series

Pirate Lords Series

Highland Outcasts

Tangled Tales Series

Lady and the Wolf (Red Riding Hood)

Just a Kiss (Frog Prince)

Beast Lord (Beauty and the Beast)

Touch of Gold (Rumpelstiltskin)

Lady in the Tower (Rapunzel)

A Perfect Fit (Cinderella)

Heart of Ice (Snow Queen)

Elemental Magick Series

The Dragon and the Dreamwalker

The Duke and the Dryad: Earth

The Sword and the Sylph: Air

The Sheik and the Siren: Water

Greek Myth Fantasy Series

Kyros' Secret

The Oracle of Delphi

The Thief of Olympus

The Pandora Curse

Once Upon a Rhyme

Mary, Mary (Mary, Mary Quite Contrary)

Muffet (Little Miss Muffet)

Blue (Little Boy Blue)

Cowboys of the Old West

The Outlaw

The Gambler

The Drifter

The Bounty Hunter

The Gunslinger

The Lawman

Dark Encounters

Familiar

The Caretaker of Showman's Hill

The Curse of the Condor

And More!

Please visit http://elizabethrosenovels.com